Merry Christmas, Darling

SERA CASSELL

Chapter One

Megan Darling loaded up the last of the evergreen boughs onto the trailer behind the tractor then wiped the sticky sap from her hands onto her flannel shirt. It was a good thing she never minded smelling like a pine tree.

After the surprise mid-November Nor'easter last week, she had spent the last two days going around Darling's Christmas Tree Farm picking up the broken branches from the trees that got knocked around in the high wind. Even though they'd lost power for a day, most of the trees on the farm weathered the storm fine. In two days, it would be Thanksgiving, which meant the day after, the busiest season for their business would start.

Meg whistled for Brody. The Australian Shepherd came out from behind a blue spruce and bounded toward her, his tongue hanging out of mouth.

He stopped in front of her and she got on her knees to rub his ears. "Chasing squirrels again?"

Brody licked her nose.

"Come on, buddy. Let's get back, it's getting dark."

He hopped into the trailer and she slid behind the steering wheel. Daylight savings time was gone, and it began to get dark around 4:30. Meg hated these shorter days but took solace in the fact that when the winter solstice arrived next month, the days would begin to get longer again.

She drove the tractor down toward the Christmas shop to drop off the boughs that she and Gran would use to make holiday wreaths and centerpieces. They had remodeled the barn into The Christmas Loft, the shop where they sold those handmade items, along with a complete inventory of everything from ornaments to Christmas tree lights.

Meg slowed the tractor as she came around the barn to see headlights of a car coming down the winding driveway. It had been plowed after the storm, but during the day the snow melted and when the sun went down it froze again. The driver hit the brakes. The car drifted sideways then careened into the snowbank in front of the Christmas Loft.

Meg winced. "Oof, that's gonna leave a mark."

She jumped down from the tractor, but Brody had already run ahead. Meg picked up her own pace, too.

The man got out of the car and promptly landed on his backside. He tried to get up and slipped again. As he attempted to stand once more Meg reached him then stuck her hand out to help him up.

"You're not from around here, are you?" she asked.

He wiped the snow from his flimsy jacket before he answered.

"No, I'm from California. I was asked to come here on behalf of my uncle, Jerome Graham."

"Jerome Graham?" Meg shuddered as she repeated the name.

"Yes, do you know him?"

Everyone in their small town of Chelsea knew *of* his uncle but no one *knew* Jerome Graham. He'd been a recluse since before Meg entered this world, according to her grandmother. And Meg bet no one even knew he had a nephew. A very handsome nephew, at that.

"I only know he lives in the mansion on the hill with the iron clad gates at the bottom of the driveway."

He drew his eyebrows together in a very serious expression. "Well, my uncle is convinced this will be his last Christmas, and he wants to throw a Christmas ball for the entire town. He'd like to purchase a few of your Christmas trees and hire you to decorate them. Well, the trees along with the rest of the house."

Meg stared into his dark brown eyes as she let what he just said sink in. Was he talking two trees? And what did he mean when he said, 'decorate them with the rest of the house.' That place was enormous.

"I'm sorry to hear about your uncle. I'm Meg, by the way."

He reached into his jacket pocket and handed her a card.

It read, Dixon Graham, Vice President, Graham Real Estate. It mentioned a California address.

"It's nice to meet you Meg. Anyway, my uncle's doctor has assured us that he isn't dying. Physically he's fine, but he did diagnose him with depression. The doctor suggested perhaps doing something to help others would make him feel better about himself, so Jerome decided to start a charity in his name. To get the word out to the community, he wishes to hold a Christmas ball at his mansion."

Meg couldn't believe it.

"Will you do it?" Dixon hunched his shoulders and dug his hands deeper into his pockets.

"It's a lot of work. What other details can you give me?"

"I'm not sure I know exactly what Jerome wants. Would it be possible to come up to the mansion tomorrow morning to meet with him?"

A hundred thoughts ran through Meg's mind, but she wouldn't refuse him. She'd always been dying to see the inside of the mansion that sat on the hill and overlooked all of Chelsea.

"Absolutely."

"Great. Now that that's settled, I'll call a tow truck to get my car out of that snowbank," he said, pulling out his cell.

As Dixon scrolled through his phone, Meg walked to the

front of the car then got down on her knees to look under it. The tires weren't buried that deep in the snow.

"I should be able to get it out for you."

Dix took his eyes away from the screen to glance at her. "I'll just call a tow company. I'm sure there's one near here, right?"

Meg raised an eyebrow. "Are you doubting my epic snow-driving skills?"

She wouldn't give him a chance to respond. She slid into the driver's seat.

"This really isn't necessary," he said.

"You might want to go stand over there," Meg pointed to the side of the barn. He raised his hands in surrender and stood where she told him.

She put the car in reverse. The tires spun a bit but when the car didn't move at all, so she threw it into drive, then into reverse, and back into drive. The car rocked back and forth a few times until she was able to back it up away from the snowbank.

She got out of the car, smiling. "You're welcome," she said.

"I think you just got lucky," he said.

"Luck had nothing to do with. That was all skill, my friend."

He finally gave her a grin.

"Well, thank you. How's nine tomorrow morning?"

"I'll be there."

He gave her a curt nod, got inside the car, and drove out of the driveway.

Meg shook her head. From the sound of it, Dixon was the only family Jerome had.

A foreign idea to Meg because she had a large extended family. Her grandparents owned and operated Darling's Tree Farm since the 50's. When her parents died in a boating accident, Meg had just turned six and her grandparents were in their 60's but they raised her. Now that they were getting on in years, Meg had taken over the running of the farm. It was the least she could do for everything they'd done for her.

She opened the back door of their old farmhouse and her

stomach growled. A pot of beef stew simmered on the stove. Smelling Gran's homemade biscuits warmed her to her toes, especially after standing in the cold talking to Dixon Graham.

Her grandfather hobbled in on his cane. "Who was that, Meg?"

She helped Pops over to his chair at the head of the table and he shooed her away. "I had a stroke. I'm not an invalid."

"You were lucky to have such a mild stroke, and I don't mind helping you."

He settled into the chair on his own. "Who was the guy in the Mercedes?"

"His name is Dixon Graham."

Her grandmother bobbled the pan of biscuits she'd just taken from the oven.

Megan raced to help her. "What happened, Gran?"

"The darn potholder slipped."

Gran began ladling the steaming stew into a soup tureen, and Meg put the biscuits in a bowl and carried them to the table.

As soon as they were all seated and started to eat, Meg said, "I guess Jerome Graham is throwing a Christmas ball because he thinks he's dying."

Pops harrumphed something unintelligible while Gran kept her eyes on her stew.

"So, what's the deal with Jerome Graham?" Meg asked.

Pops grabbed his second biscuit and spread it with butter. "You mean other than Jerry being the loser in our love triangle?"

"Heathcliff!"

"I won't lie to the girl, Evie. Besides, if Jerry is having a shindig at that mansion of his, it's bound to come out."

"Whoa, wait. The three of you were in a love triangle, and you chose Pops?"

"That's right, Meg," Pops gloated. "And Jerry never got over it."

Gran just shoveled spoonful after spoonful of stew into her mouth without saying a word to confirm or deny Pops' story.

They ate the rest of their meal in awkward silence, the only sound coming from their spoons clinking on the china bowls.

"What did this Dixon want with you?" Pops asked, as Gran began to clear the table.

"Jerome wants me to decorate the whole mansion for the ball he's giving."

"I'm sure he needs all the help he can get."

"Cliff, that's enough."

Megan startled at the tone of Gran's voice. Her sainted grandmother never raised her voice, but all this talk about the town recluse got her ire up.

Pops mumbled under his breath and hobbled back into the living room, leaving Megan alone with Gran, who kept her attention on loading the dishwasher.

"So?" Megan asked. "Are you going to fill me in?"

Her grandmother straightened and huffed out a breath. "I don't suppose you'll stop pestering me until I do."

Meg scrubbed the soup pot in the sink. "Not a chance. I've lived in this small town my whole life. If even part of what Pops said is true, I need you to spill it. Just let me rinse this so I don't miss a word."

They finished cleaning up from dinner and Gran brought over the cake she'd made earlier. As she started to frost it, she inhaled a deep breath.

"Your grandfather and I went to high school together. In our senior year, Jerome's family moved into town. He was handsome, and it was obvious his family had more money than anyone else in town. All the girls wanted Jerome to ask them to the homecoming dance."

"Wait, don't tell me. He asked you."

A huge smile lit up Gran's face. "He did."

Megan was sure she'd never seen Gran blush.

"I'm guessing the other girls were jealous," Meg said.

"They were. After the dance, he asked me to go steady. Back then, going steady meant he held my hand, and we went to the drug store for root beer floats. Nobody hopped into bed with each other the day after they met the way you kids do nowadays."

Megan laughed. She'd never hopped into bed after just meeting anyone, but whatever. "So why did you break up with him?"

"I didn't. The Korean War happened. Jerome got drafted. The night before he had to leave, he took me to the beach and asked me to marry him. I said yes."

"That sounds so romantic."

"It was. The girls in town tried to say I was after his money, but I ignored them. I only wanted was what my parents had—a loving marriage. Jerome wanted that too."

Megan watched as Gran stuck the spatula in the ceramic bowl, dug out a glob of frosting, and spread it up the side of the cake.

"Where does Pops fit into the picture?"

"Heathcliff was his parent's only son. His father had just passed, and his mother needed him here to run the farm, so he never left. Betrothed to Jerome, I waited for the war to end so we could start our life together, until his family got a letter saying that he got killed in action."

Meg's heart dropped. "But—"

"Yes, the government made a mistake. There was more than one Jerome Graham and they sent the letter to the wrong family."

Gran left the table and filled the kettle for tea. Megan grappled with what her grandmother had just told her.

A few minutes later Gran returned, carrying two steaming mugs. Meg stuck her nose in the steam to smell the sweet Chamomile then glanced back up at her. "I don't understand. If he was alive why are you married to Pops?"

"It took the government several months to realize their mistake. By then my world had ended. I was heartbroken and became depressed. My father hired Heathcliff to help him with odd jobs around the house. At least that's what he told me. I think he hated watching me grieve and hoped Heathcliff would be a distraction."

Megan reached across the table and squeezed Gran's hand. "It worked, right? You married him."

"We courted for a little while and he asked me to marry him. Part of me still believed Jerome was still alive, but my mother convinced me that war changed a man and even if Jerome hadn't died, he'd be different. I married Heathcliff a few months later. Soon after that Jerome came back home."

Meg's chest tightened imagining how Gran felt when she saw Jerome for the first time after she married another man. The heartache they both endured must have been crushing.

"But you loved Pops, right?"

Gran sipped her tea and didn't answer right away. "Love isn't always so black and white, Meg. I battled my own civil war between my heart and head."

"I don't understand."

"The heart wants what the heart wants, right? Obviously, I married Heathcliff," Gran continued. "But when Jerome turned up amongst the living, it threw me. I struggled with my decision and well, Jerome was miserable."

Meg tried to put herself in her grandmother's shoes. "Your heart must've been torn in two. How did you manage it?"

"I didn't have to. Your grandfather did the most noble thing. He offered to divorce me so Jerome and I could be together."

Her grandfather had always been a very proud and honest man. He had always prided himself on using sound logic and reason to solve any problem. But offering to divorce Gran to be with someone else, went above and beyond anything a man should have to do.

Tears pricked her eyes, thinking about the sad situation they'd all been put in.

"That's so romantic."

"Romance had nothing to do with it," Pops said, making his way back into the kitchen. "I didn't want to live my life with a woman who regretted marrying me and would spend her life pining for another man."

He sat in his chair and Gran cut him a piece of cake.

"But you loved Gran, right?"

"With every ounce of my being. But love isn't any good if it's one-sided."

"He's right, Meg. When we're talking hearts, it takes two halves to make a whole."

Meg understood that better than anyone. It had been a year since Josh left her at the altar leaving a giant crater in her own heart.

Gran cut two more pieces of cake. She gave Meg one then sat down next to Pops with her own. Pops winked up at Gran and she smiled, patting his hand.

That little show of affection between them caused emotion to bubble up inside her. She swallowed against the tightness in her throat and fought back tears. Meg hated that she might never have that.

"What a great story," she finally said.

"Oh, Meg," Gran said, hearing her hoarse voice from the emotion stuck in her larynx. "You will find someone who loves you the way you deserved to be loved."

Meg nodded. Gran meant well, but Meg wouldn't grant anyone access to her heart for a long time, if ever.

"So, the mansion belonged to Jerome's family?" Meg asked, changing the subject.

"No, Jerome demolished his family's house to build that mansion," Pops said. "The family home was a normal looking house near the road. Jerome built the mansion on the hill for Evie's sake."

Meg licked the frosting off her fork. "Why?"

"So, every time she looked up at his fine-looking house, she'd regret marrying me."

Gran sat back in the chair.

"But I never have. My mother was right. Jerome changed.

Whether it was the effects of war or the fact that I married your grandfather, he became bitter. It was unfortunate what had happened to us, but God had another plan, I guess."

Her grandparents went back to eating their cake and sipping their drinks.

Jerome Graham stayed single because of the gaping hole in his heart left by Gran. And while it wasn't Gran's fault, the circumstances sucked. Meg had never met the recluse that lived on the hill, but at least she understood why he chose to live like that. Her heart still ached from Josh leaving her while she waited in the back of the packed church on that humid August day. Time lessened the pain, but she had to wonder if it would ever completely go away.

"I'm glad the two of you got together, otherwise, I wouldn't be here. But Jerome never finding love again? That's like a Shakespeare tragedy."

"Life is all about choices, Meg. As Evie said, he was miserable, and he's got no one to blame but himself."

Pops finished his cake then headed back into the living room. Megan took her plate to the sink and leaned up against the counter to finish her tea.

"Well, I hope Mr. Graham isn't a crotchety old man when I meet with him. Why don't you come with me and be my buffer?"

"Oh God, no," Gran gave a dismissive wave. "We have nothing to say to each other. I wouldn't be much of a buffer."

Meg wouldn't force the issue. It would be awkward for all of them.

She kissed Gran's cheek. "If he does ask about you, can I tell him you send your best?"

"You can, but he won't."

Meg would just have to wait and see on that.

Chapter Two

The next morning, Dix walked into the library of his uncle's mansion to see his eight-year-old son Noah, and Megan Darling on all fours under the antique roll-top desk.

"There it is," Meg cried out to Noah, who crawled around with her.

Dix cleared his throat as he glanced down at Uncle Jerome in his motorized wheelchair next to him. He blinked once, then twice.

Jerome wore a semblance of a smile.

Noah and Meg backed out from under the desk. The second Noah saw them, he stood at attention with perfect posture and didn't move while Meg held a muffin in her hand. She nudged his son with her elbow.

"Great job, kid," she said before glancing over to Dix. "I was buttering my muffin when it slipped out of my hand and rolled away."

Noah kept his eyes forward, but Dix saw the beginnings of a smile playing on his son's lips. He returned his attention to her and thought about her reason for being there.

At eighty-five, his uncle was finally getting treated for his depression. For fifty or so years his mansion overlooked the town of Chelsea where he lived in seclusion. He'd never married and the only family he had was Dix's father, Jerome's younger brother. It was Jerome's idea to start a charity and to kick it off, he'd host a Christmas ball in his home.

When Dix met Megan the day before, she was dressed like a lumberjack, wearing a flannel jacket, jeans, and work boots, while her hair had been tucked up inside one of those hats with flaps over the ears and turned up at the forehead. Today she dressed in a sweater, a skirt, and black dress boots. Her long, blond hair, free from the confines of the hat, rested in waves down her back.

"Megan Darling, I believe you already met my nephew, Dixon," Jerome said.

Dix reached over, took her hand in his, and gave it a squeeze. "Yes. Megan helped me get your car out of that snowbank."

He had mentioned the incident to his uncle worried that he might've done some sort of damage to the car. He offered to pay if he had.

Jerome nodded. "Enough of this small talk. We have much to discuss. Have a seat, Miss Darling."

"Call me Meg. Is it okay if I call you Jerry?"

Jerry? Dix snickered under his breath. Megan had a lot to learn about—

"I'd like that," his uncle said surprising Dix again.

Megan walked around the desk to sit in the chair and Jerome moved his scooter next to her.

Noah hadn't moved from his spot since he came out from under the desk proving that his high-priced boarding school education was well worth the money.

Megan and Jerome settled in to chat about the Christmas ball, which they didn't need Dix for. He turned for the door when Megan whistled as if she called for her dog.

"Aren't you forgetting something?" She jerked her head toward Noah, who remained still like a toy soldier.

"Oh, right. You may go, Noah."

Noah relaxed his shoulders. "Can I stay here to help Meg and Uncle Jerome with the ball?"

Dixon opened his mouth to protest.

"Of course, you can," Megan said. "I'm going to need someone to help me pick out the trees and decorate them."

"That's what my uncle is paying you to do," Dix said. And damn good money, too.

Meg kept the smile on her face. "I could use an extra hand if Noah doesn't mind."

"For God's sake, Dixon, Christmas is for kids. Let the boy help," Jerome spat.

Dix fought a losing battle with the two of them. Noah lowered his head to hide the fact that he chuckled.

"Fine. Noah, you will maintain your best behavior."

Megan rolled her eyes. "He'll be fine. Right, Bud?"

Noah grinned openly now. "Right."

He had no idea how she managed it, but an hour later when Megan Darling left the mansion, she had turned the broody mood of Graham manor merry and bright with Christmas spirit.

By the time Megan left Graham mansion, she'd planned Jerry's entire Christmas ball and left an open invitation for the Graham family to join her and the rest of the Darling family for Thanksgiving dinner. She couldn't help it. When she stood to leave, Noah and Jerry looked like they'd just lost their best friend, and it tugged on her heartstrings.

On the other hand, Dixon wore a stone-faced, stick-up-his-butt expression when she extended the invite. Meg doubted they'd show up, which made her blood boil thinking how much fun Noah could be having at the Darlings' with other kids his age.

She walked through the back door of the farmhouse and the savory fragrance of sage and rosemary tickled her nose. At the stove, Gran prepared the stuffing that would go into their turkey during the pre-dawn hours of Thanksgiving morning.

"Smells like Thanksgiving," Meg said, kissing Gran's cheek. "I'll change and start the cranberry relish."

Meg ran upstairs, got out of her dressy clothes, and threw on a pair of yoga pants with a sweatshirt. Back in the kitchen, she got the cranberries out of the fridge, grabbed a couple of oranges from the fruit bowl on the counter, and brought everything to the table.

"So how is Jerome?" Gran asked.

"He's okay. He's starting a charity and wants to have this ball to kick it off. He's inviting the entire town."

Gran tugged on the bag of croutons too hard and it split down the side. Croutons flew out all over the counter and the floor.

"Yikes, Gran. You don't know your own strength. Let me help you."

She picked up the croutons from the floor and threw them in the trash.

"My strength has nothing to do with it, Meg. The fact that Jerome Graham is going to allow people into that mansion of his is nothing short of a miracle."

Meg grabbed a bowl from the cabinet then pulled the old-fashioned food grinder from the under the sink, fastening it to the edge of the table like a vise. She could've used the food processor she'd bought Gran a few years ago, but somehow the old hand crank grinder gave Meg a sense of nostalgia from her childhood. Since her parent's accident in 1999, she spent the day before Thanksgiving preparing the meal with Gran, just like this. No sense in changing her ways now.

"Well, I'm glad he's finally going to socialize with others," Gran said. "He wouldn't be so depressed if he occasionally came out of that prison he built for himself," she added.

Meg picked the rotten cranberries out of the bowl before dumping the good ones into the grinder.

"Well, it's a beautiful prison and just for the record, it has no bars on the windows. There are sparkly chandeliers in the foyer and dining room. Oriental carpets over gleaming, dark hardwood floors. I never made it to the kitchen, but I'm guessing it's just as amazing."

"Oh, I'm sure it has everything." Gran stirred the croutons into the pan of simmering broth and stirred with a wooden spoon.

"Yep, he's even got a complete kitchen staff. Too bad the entire place stinks of desperation and loneliness."

The kitchen grew quiet except for the sound of Meg grinding the cranberries and Gran chopping at the counter. The silence grew louder, something Meg always hated.

"When Pops offered you the option to go back to Jerome after you guys were already married, what did you think, Gran?"

"I knew I had found true love. Your grandfather was willing to give up everything for me to be happy. I've been here for over sixty years and have never regretted my decision to stay."

Meg nodded. True love was about sacrifice and devotion, yet sometimes it came at a price. She'd been lucky to be raised by the two of them where she got to see that every day.

"You guys have a great story," she said.

Gran shook her head. "Everything worked out for us. But each time I look up the hill and see that mansion, it makes me angry that Jerome has lived there alone when he could've filled it up with children and grandchildren. I think your grandfather and I were married about four years when I decided he needed to hear a few things."

Megan stirred the sugar into the cranberries. "So, you ripped him a new one, huh?"

"Well, no, but we did have a heart-to-heart talk. I urged him to find someone to share his life with, and he told me he couldn't. He said he wanted me, and no one would ever compare."

"That's so sweet."

"No, Meg. That's selfish and boorish. I told him he was acting like a three-year-old throwing a tantrum because he couldn't have what he wanted."

"And what did he say?"

"He disagreed, of course. He said he was waiting for me to come to my senses and leave Heathcliff. That everything he built, everything he did in that house, he did for me."

Pops hobbled into the kitchen, no doubt overhearing their conversation and having something to add.

"What did you think about 'ol Jerry still making the moves on Gran?"

"He was and always will be a damn fool."

Meg tasted the relish and the tang of the cranberries made her shiver. It definitely needed more sugar.

"Well, foolish or not, he looked genuinely sorry when I told him about your stroke," Meg said.

After more sugar and one more taste, Meg deemed the relish delicious. She grabbed another spoon from the drawer and gave Pops a taste.

"What do you think?" she asked.

"It needs more sugar."

"I'm sure it's fine," Gran said. "He'll have you add the entire five-pound bag if he has his way."

Megan brought the bowl of relish to the counter to cover it with plastic wrap and placed it in the fridge.

"Have you ever wondered what your life would've been like if you didn't marry Pops and married Jerry instead?"

"Never. Thoughts like that are what get marriages in trouble."

Pops nodded and started to stand. Meg skipped over to him to help, and he batted her hand.

"Just trying to help," she said.

"I know, but I hate having to depend on this damn cane or anyone else to get around."

As her grandfather left the room, Meg said, "Well, I hope you guys don't mind, but I invited Jerry, his nephew Dixon, and Dixon's son, Noah for Thanksgiving dinner."

"You what?" Pops glared at her.

"Don't worry, Cliff. He won't come," Gran said. "But if his nephews decide to join us, we'll have plenty. I don't know how to cook for less than an army."

No truer words had ever been spoken in the Darling house.

For the rest of the day, Meg helped Gran prepare for Thanksgiving. Early the next morning, Meg rounded the corner from the living room to the kitchen to see Gran struggle with the giant turkey in the equally giant roasting pan.

"Stop. Put the bird down slowly and no one gets hurt."

Gran chuckled. "I guess I overstuffed this sucker."

Meg lifted the pan while Gran hurried to open the oven door.

Once the turkey was safely inside, Meg pushed her hair under the beanie Gran had crocheted her, headed out to the chicken coop, and wondered if Dixon Graham and his son would show up later for dinner.

Chapter Three

D ixon sat at one end of the long dining room table with Noah to his left, while Jerome sat at the other end. Noah pushed his scrambled eggs around on his plate the way he had been for the last five minutes.

"Noah, eat your eggs."

"I'm not that hungry. May I be excused?" Noah asked.

"Can't you tell the boy is bored out of his mind?" his uncle bellowed. "Isn't there a parade on the television he should be watching?"

Noah's head snapped toward Dixon.

"Do you want to watch the Thanksgiving Day parade?" Dix asked. With no video games around, what else was there for him to do?

Noah bobbed his head up and down.

"You may be excused." It was a holiday, after all.

Noah left the dining room while Dix looked down at the other end of the table, turning his attention back to Jerome who sipped on his orange juice and also pushed his eggs around.

"So, what's your excuse for not eating? Are you bored, too?" Dix wiped his mouth on the linen napkin.

"I don't have much of an appetite these days."

"And why do you suppose that is?"

When Megan Darling arrived a day ago, Jerome's usual pasty white pallor had changed. His eyes had brightened, and his cheeks had color in them. Today his uncle looked washed out again.

If Dix hadn't talked with Jerome's doctor, he too would've thought his uncle ill. But the doctor assured Dix that Jerome was in good health physically. His mental state, however, needed some work. It had been the reason for hosting a charity ball, and after speaking with his lawyers and accountants, Jerome decided to set up a foundation in his name to help various charities.

"Do I have to take up Megan Darling on her invitation to attend Thanksgiving dinner with her family?" Dix teased.

"Why do you say that?"

"Because you never looked better than when Meg was here."

Jerome picked up his head and stared down the table at him.

"She reminds me of Evelyn Darling."

His voice broke and Dix's stomach tightened for bringing it up in the first place.

Dix had no idea what the details of his relationship between Megan's grandmother and his uncle were, but he could venture a guess that Jerome lost his heart to her.

"Are you single, Dixon?" Jerome asked.

Dix pushed his plate away and took a sip of coffee before he answered.

"I am, and I like it that way."

"But you were married once. Tell me what she was like."

"That was a long time ago."

Jerome narrowed his eyes. "They say that time makes you forget certain things about a person. But I can still remember what it felt like to hold Evie's hand and see her smile reach her blue eyes. There's got to be something you remember about your ex."

Dix tried hard to remember. "She was..." Dix's voice trailed off as he thought about how Karen had changed dramatically after she gave birth to Noah.

Jerome raised a questioning brow. "What?"

"She wasn't who I thought she was. We were very young, and, in the end, we wanted different things."

"Was she after your money? Is that it?"

Dix fidgeted in his seat and took a deep breath. He hated being put on the spot and he detested thinking about Karen and the way she left him.

"Did she take you for everything you've got?" Jerome pressed.

"No. She wanted out of the marriage and the raising of our son. I made it as easy as possible for her to leave."

"What about the boy? Does she ever call or come around for him?"

"No."

If Karen had her way, she would have aborted the pregnancy altogether. It was only because Dix bribed her with cash that she agreed to marry him and stay on for two years. He hoped during that time she would change her mind. That she would've wanted to be a family and realize what he could provide for her and Noah. But the day after Noah's second birthday, she left.

"I'm sorry to hear that," Jerome said and sounded like he meant it. "Love is a sneaky bastard."

"Care to explain that?"

"It's what kept me alive during the war. Love for Evie and all we had planned once I got back. But love has a way of leading you down a well-lit path only to cast you back into the shadows. I was gutted when I came back home to find out she'd already married Heathcliff Darling. That pain had been greater than all the months of starving and being beaten while being a prisoner. And it lasted for much, much longer."

Dix understood the moral of Jerome's story. Love could be a double-edged sword. You must put your heart out there. Once you do, it gets battered, war-torn. But love can't be won unless you do exactly that. And like Jerome, he wasn't sure if he ever wanted to do it again.

"I had no idea," Dix said.

"Of course not. It's not something I ever talk about."

"Why are you telling me now?"

"I never had children of my own. You are the closest thing I have to that and someone should know if for no other reason than for posterity's sake."

Jerome's sigh could be heard from across the table. "Speaking of kids, the boy tells me he's in boarding school."

"He is. I didn't want to be bothered with the whole nanny thing and it's been good for discipline."

Jerome nodded then finished his orange juice. "Did you go to boarding school?"

"I went to a prestigious high school that was also a boarding school, yes."

"But when you were younger, you were allowed to go outside with your friends?"

"Yes, but times are different now."

Dix thought of the affluent neighborhood he grew up in and how he and his friends would play in the brook that ran through their backyards. He came in covered in mud on a nightly basis, much to his mother's dismay.

"I don't think that's true," Jerome said. "I grew up throwing snowballs and making snowmen, learning to play hockey on the frozen pond in the back yard, sledding down the hill on the other side of the orchard. In summer, my friends and I would ride our bicycles, swim and fish in that pond. That's what I would've wanted for my own kids."

Jerome's life story could've been something from a Dickens novel, yet it made him understand why his uncle had become such an ornery old man. Dix pushed his chair back.

"Is there a point to your story, Uncle?"

"There is." Jerome drew his eyebrows together and pointed a knobby finger at him.

"You send the boy away because he reminds you of the wife you lost, and you've locked up your heart. I did that when I built this place to spite Evie. In the end, I only hurt myself. Don't do what I did. Find love again and bring the boy home from that boarding school so he's raised by a mother and a father who love him."

Jerome backed his motorized wheelchair away from the table and left the dining room.

Dix leaned back in his seat and stared at the ceiling. All he ever wanted was to be a family. But he and Karen were only twenty when she got pregnant. Having a child didn't fit into her future, she'd said. She only hung around the two years after Noah's birth for the payout he'd promised.

She blamed him for everything. For making her have the baby and destroying her life. She'd never been in love with him or their child. He swallowed past the wet lump in his throat, remembering how she slung those barbed words at him. How they stuck in his heart.

After she left, Dix had no choice but to accept her decision. He did what he had to do for Noah. He moved in with his parents and they helped raise his son. But the love he'd had for Karen left a bitter taste in his mouth. For that reason alone, he wouldn't allow anyone else to ever get close to his heart again.

Later, Dix descended the winding staircase to find Noah sitting on the floor in front of the television.

"How's the parade?"

"Okay, I guess."

"Is there something else you want to watch?" Dix asked.

"Not really."

Dix glanced out the window. The sun shone brightly on the town of Chelsea and Thanksgiving dinner wouldn't be served until two. They had five hours to kill.

"Want to go for a ride?"

Noah jumped up. "Where?"

"I don't know. Grab your coat."

Dix still had the keys to Jerome's Mercedes in his jacket pocket. The two hopped in, and he took off down the driveway through the open gates.

After checking the chicken coop for eggs and feeding her horses, Meg walked over to the Christmas Loft, to check the tree bailer. The other day it seemed fine, but a double-check wouldn't hurt seeing as though the day after Thanksgiving was the busiest day at the farm.

Just as she finished, a car door slammed, and Brody began to bark. Meg came around the side of the Christmas Loft, and Noah Graham threw himself at her, almost knocking her over.

He threw his arms around her waist, and she wrapped her arms around him. She barely knew the kid, but after spending a little time with him, Dix, and Jerry at the mansion, Meg sensed there wasn't a lot of open affection between them. The way the kid hugged her, told her as much.

"Hey, Noah. Happy Thanksgiving."

"Hi, Meg. My Dad and I were driving around, and I asked if we could stop by. Is it okay?"

"Of course, it's okay."

Meg glanced up to see Dixon in his usual pole-up-the-butt posture wearing a grimace.

"Hi, Dix."

"Hi. I hope we're not interrupting," he said, his teeth chattering.

"Not at all. You look cold."

He nodded and dug his hands deep into the pockets of his blue jeans. Jeans that looked pressed.

"Follow me," Meg said and opened the door to the Christmas Loft. She strode around the counter and grabbed Pops' heavy coat that hung on a hook behind it and brought it to Dix.

"Here."

"What's this?"

Meg looked over at Noah. "Is this guy for real?"

Noah shrugged. "I'm afraid so."

"It's called a winter coat, silly. You're going to need it when we walk over to the barn. How old are you, Noah?"

"Eight, almost nine."

"Yeah, you need to stop talking like a forty-year-old man and more like a kid. Come on. Let's go see the horses."

His face lit up. "Yes, I'd like that."

"No, kid. You're supposed to say, 'that's cool', or, 'awesome.'"

Noah laughed but didn't repeat her words.

They began their trek from the Christmas Loft to the barn by way of the chicken coop and the snow-covered pumpkin patch. Meg loved the crisp morning air against her cheeks and the way she could see her breath.

Noah ran up ahead to get a closer look at the chickens. Dixon opened his mouth to shout at him, but Meg placed her hand on his arm. Dix glanced down at her hand there and lifted a brow. She quickly removed it.

"Sorry. I'm a toucher. Can't help it. Don't worry about Noah, he's fine. Farms are made for kids to run around and have fun."

"Yes, but if he gets overstimulated, it takes a lot to settle him down."

"I have a cure for that."

"You do?"

"Mucking out the stables. It's the best remedy."

From what she knew of the guy, which wasn't much, he took life a little too seriously. Would it kill him to smile?

"How's Jerry today? Do you think he'll come down for dinner?"

Dix shook his head. "I don't think so. Do you know about him and your grandmother?"

"I do. Crazy, right?"

"It is. I don't know how I would've handled the situation. I can't imagine Uncle Jerome being romantic with anyone."

Meg nodded in agreement. "Neither can I, but I for one appreciate it when a guy is romantic. I'm sure your wife likes it, too."

"I don't have a wife, and I'm not looking for one."

"Direct and to the point. I like it." Megan took his hint and changed the subject. "Well, just for the record, Noah is the best-behaved kid I've ever met."

"Thank you, but I can't take the credit. The headmaster at his boarding school is responsible for that."

Meg stopped in her tracks. "Wait. He doesn't live with you?"

"He lives at a private school in Northern California."

Meg would keep her opinions to herself.

"I can see you don't approve," Dix said.

"It's also not my business. I just know, if I had kids, I'd want to be the one to raise them. But hey, that's me. I'll shut my mouth now."

She slid her fingers across her lips in a zipper motion and threw away a make-believe key.

They approached the chicken coop and Noah ran up to Meg. "Where are the eggs?"

"There were only three this morning and I already took them inside. The cold weather slows down the laying process."

"Can I come over to help you sometime?"

"Noah," Dix warned.

"Only if you can be here around 6:30 in the morning," she said.

Dix shoved a hand threw his hair and winced.

"Looks like we'll have to work on your Dad, Noah. Let's go check on the horses."

Noah and Brody ran up ahead.

"What do you do with all your free time, if Noah's away at school?"

"I manage my family's real estate business." He stopped and glared at her again. "Are you playing twenty questions?"

"Maybe," she chuckled. "I'll stop if I'm making you uncomfortable. I think it comes from living in a small town and everyone knowing everyone else's business. But turnabout is fair play. You're welcome to ask me some questions."

"I only have one. How did you get my uncle to laugh for the first time in years?"

Megan sighed. This guy just didn't get it.

"I just treat people the way I want to be treated."

"That doesn't explain how you got him to crack a smile."

They entered the barn and found Noah feeding hay to Sam.

"I really don't know. Your uncle has an air of sadness around him. I only tried to bring in some levity."

They walked into the barn. While Dix wrinkled up his nose, Meg smiled. The sweet hay mingled with the earthy scent of manure smelled like home, but she'd grown up with it. Obviously, Dix hadn't.

Noah stood in front of one of the stalls.

"I see you've met Sam. That's his brother, Dean in the next stall."

Dixon drew his brows together. "Sam and Dean?"

"Yeah. After the brothers in one of my favorite T.V. shows."

They spent a while in the barn. Meg showed Noah how to brush the horses and gave him a quick lesson in mucking out a stall before she saw Dixon check his fancy, gold watch.

"We have to get back, Noah," Dix said.

Noah made a frowny face, but unlike most kids his age who would've talked back, he kept his mouth closed and followed them out of the barn back toward the Christmas Loft.

"Well, don't forget, there's an open invitation for you to join us for dinner or dessert."

Noah gave his father a hopeful expression, and Dix shook his head.

"Thanks, but I can't leave Jerome alone."

"I understand. Well, maybe you can talk Jerome into coming for dessert."

"I wouldn't count on it."

Dix handed her Pop's coat, and she gave Noah a hug.

"I'll see you guys around. Come on, Brody."

The Grahams drove away, and Meg ran with Brody to the back door and inside.

"A visit from the Grahams?" Gran asked while basting the turkey.

"Yeah. Noah said they were out on a ride. He asked Dix to stop here."

"Any idea what Dixon's story is?"

Meg poured herself a cup of coffee. "Not really, but he's brutally honest, I'll give him that. He told me in no uncertain terms he does not have a wife or girlfriend and he's not interested in finding one. And get this. Noah goes to a boarding school. Can you imagine that?"

Gran shoved the turkey back in the oven and shut the door.

"No, but then again, we never had that kind of money."

Meg swiped a donut from the tray on the counter and took a bite, the cinnamon and sugar coating sweet on her taste buds.

She pointed the half-eaten donut at Gran. "Dixon only talked about how well-behaved Noah is and how the school teaches discipline. Yet that kid hugged me as if his life depended on it. He needs to be loved, Gran."

Gran tsked softly. "It sounds like his father needs to be loved, too."

"You're probably, right, but it won't be from me."

"Why is that?"

"He's not my type. He only cares about expensive cars, clothes, and fancy jewelry. And he lives in California."

Gran stirred creamer into her coffee and said, "You know, Meg, I'm a firm believer in people entering our lives to teach us lessons."

Meg snorted. "What lesson could Dixon Graham need to teach me?"

"It's not what he can teach you. It's what you can do for him and his young son."

"Gran, I know you and Pops want me to get married and live

happily ever after, but I'm fine being single." She kissed Gran's soft cheek. "Really, I am."

"You keep telling yourself that, Meg. I happen to know otherwise."

Gran never pried, but always spoke her mind. Sometimes Meg listened but other times, she chose to ignore her. Like now.

"I'm washing up then we'll tackle peeling that giant bag of potatoes," Meg said.

"Okay, but you mark my words. That family needs to be rescued and you might just be the one to do it."

Chapter Four

Dix found his uncle in the library in his motorized wheelchair staring out the window. As he stood behind him, he understood why Jerome sat there. The view overlooked Darling's Farm.

"Where did you go?" his uncle asked.

"Down there, to visit Meg."

Jerome nodded but kept his gaze to the window. "Did you meet Evie?"

"No, but Meg's invitation for dinner and dessert is still open."

Jerome spun his scooter around away from the window.

"You should take the boy and go." He sped to the door.

"I won't leave you alone on Thanksgiving."

"I'm not alone. I make the staff join me. Go, have a good time. Tell me all about it when you come back."

The entire reason for coming east was to spend the holidays with Jerome. Dix opened his mouth to refuse then thought of Noah. He'd been bored hanging around the mansion. And Jerome had insisted that they go.

"Are you sure?" Dix asked.

"I wouldn't have suggested it if I wasn't. Noah should be with kids his own age, and the Darlings have quite the extended family."

Dix couldn't argue. "I guess it's settled then. Would you like me to take pictures to show you when we return?"

"I'll leave that up to you."

At the Darlings, Noah rang the doorbell. The older gentleman who answered it stood there, leaning on a cane.

"Can I help you?" he growled.

"Hi. This is Noah and I'm Dixon Graham. Meg–"

"Graham?"

The man he assumed was Megan's grandfather opened his mouth to continue, but Megan swooped in and saved them before the older man had the chance.

"Pops, you're being rude to our guests."

"Guests?"

"I invited them, remember?"

Mr. Darling glowered and shuffled off to another room.

"Sorry about that. Do you still want to come in?" She grinned.

Noah answered yes and pushed past Dix before he had a chance to say anything.

"My cousins are in the kitchen helping Gran make the appetizers if you want to help them," Meg said to Noah. "Head to the room with the most noise." The kid took off his coat, handed it to Meg, and headed toward the back of the house.

Meg took Dix's coat too and hung them up on the coat tree near the door.

"You couldn't talk Jerry into coming, huh?"

Dix shook his head. "No, but he insisted that I come with Noah."

"Come on, I'll introduce you to Gran."

Megan slid her hand into his to tug him along behind her and his heart kicked, pushing warmth through his extremities. The unfamiliar sensation made him uncomfortable. He quickly pulled his hand out of hers and placed it in his jeans pocket. If it bothered Meg, she didn't give him any inkling.

They entered the kitchen and Noah had already rolled up his sleeves and helped tear a head of lettuce into bite-sized pieces alongside two other kids that looked to be around the same age.

"Gran, this is Dixon Graham. Dix, meet my grandmother, Evelyn Darling."

The older woman had pretty blue eyes, the same that Jerome had spoken about. They lightened even more when she smiled, and Dix immediately could see how Jerome had fallen for her. She exuded a kindness that put him at ease.

Evelyn wiped her hands on the towel that hung from her shoulder before shaking his hand.

"Welcome, Dixon. I see you couldn't convince that old coot to join us?"

Dix couldn't help but snicker at her comment. "No."

"Don't just stand there, Meg," Evie said. "Get Dixon a drink."

Megan motioned for him to follow her to the refrigerator. She looked inside and began rattling off a list. "We've got beer, wine, eggnog, soda, and sparkling water. If you want whiskey or anything harder, we have that too, out in the dining room. Name your poison."

"I'll have that bottle of sparkling water."

He pointed to a green bottle behind a jar of pickles.

She reached in, pulled it out, and handed it to him.

"You actually drink this stuff?"

"Isn't that why you had it in there?" He twisted off the top and took a sip.

"We usually add it to fruit juice to make spritzers. Must be a California thing."

They all startled when the back door slammed open and a little girl, who Dix guessed to be about three or four-years-old, ran through it.

"A little help please," a young woman called through the screen door. Meg ran over, opened the door, and retrieved the pie the women balanced precariously in one hand while holding a car seat with a screaming infant in the other.

Dix leaned against the kitchen counter taking in all the commotion. The child ran to Evelyn. The two hugged both excited to see each other. While Evie helped the child off with her pink coat, Meg placed the pie on the counter near the stove and went back to the car seat chatting with the young woman while undoing the complicated series of belts and lifting out the crying baby.

Meg undressed the baby out of a snowsuit, a boy judging from all the blue he wore, then picked up a pacifier from the seat and stuck it in his mouth. She cradled him in her arms and lightly bounced up and down. In between the conversation with the other woman, she placed tender kisses on the baby's forehead. All her bouncing and rocking worked. The baby stopped screaming and order got restored to the controlled chaos around them.

The beginning of a smile tugged up at the corners of his lips as he watched her, and he had no idea why. He knew nothing about her, yet being there, he did have questions. For starters, she lived with her grandparents but had never mentioned her parents. He saw no wedding ring, so guessed she was not married, and judging by the way she fussed over the baby and earlier spoke about raising her kids herself, she wanted children.

Megan beamed as she held the baby close to her chest and half-walked, half-rocked toward him.

"Dixon Graham, meet Colton Elijah Darling."

"Congratulations," Dix said, glancing at Colton's mother.

"Thank you. I'm Leia."

"Dix is visiting his uncle," Meg said, "in the mansion on the hill."

"The Graham mansion?" Leia's eyes widened.

"Yes," Dix said.

The baby started fussing again and no amount of rocking quieted him down.

"He's hungry," Leia said taking the baby. "I'll be back."

She left the kitchen and the back door opened again. This

time a guy entered carrying a diaper bag and a host of other baby paraphernalia.

"Here, let me get that for you." Dix did the polite thing and ran over to help him.

"Thanks. The baby has more gear than I do. Matt Darling."

Dix shook his hand. "Dixon Graham." The expression on Matt's face told Dix he didn't have to explain who he was.

"No kidding. How are you related to old man Graham?"

"He's my uncle."

"Huh. I never knew the guy had any family."

"He does. Not as big as yours, though."

Matt laughed. "Which one of my family members invited you?"

Megan returned to Dix's side.

"That would be me. And Gran. She invited Jerome Graham, too, but he refused."

Matt's eyebrows shot up. "Wow. Hey, excuse me while I go say hi to Gran and Pops."

"Are you overwhelmed yet?" Megan asked.

"Not yet. How many more family members are coming?"

"I'm not sure. Probably between fifteen and twenty, give or take a few."

He thought she was kidding. She wasn't.

By the time they all sat down to dinner, Dix counted twenty-six, not including himself or Noah. The guests ranged in ages from two months to eighty-five. For the first time since he'd met Megan, he was grateful she sat next to him, being the one person, he actually knew.

For dinner, they had everything from turkey and cranberry sauce to green bean casserole and sweet potatoes with marshmallows on top. But what amazed him the most was what happened after dinner. No one left. They all sat at the table talking and laughing.

Every family dinner he'd ever attended at home he did so out of obligation.

The Darling family genuinely enjoyed spending this time together, a foreign concept to him.

Leia stood near the table rocking Colton and eating with one hand. Meg got up, took the baby, and insisted Leia sit to enjoy her meal. Dix's gaze tangled with Meg's and she motioned with her head for him to join her in the other room.

Noah had already gone off with the other boys to the family room, so Dix politely excused himself and followed Meg.

"Sorry about my noisy family," she said.

Dix went over to the fireplace to look at the family pictures on the mantle. He picked up a picture of a little girl riding a horse, wearing a helmet, and a toothless smile.

"There's no need to apologize. Is this you?"

"I was like seven in that picture. After my parents died, Pops thought I should have something to take my mind off things, so he bought me a horse."

His heart fell. He never imagined the reason she lived here with Evie and her grandfather was that her parents died.

"I'm sorry to hear that."

Megan shrugged and switched Colton from the crook of her left arm to the crook of her right. "I was six when it happened. They both drowned in a boating accident. I'm lucky I had Gran and Pops."

He put the picture back and watched her with Colton. She bent down and lightly brushed her lips over his little forehead.

Megan picked up her head, and Dix's breath got hung up somewhere between his chest and his throat. Caught in the undertow, he found himself struggling. He wanted to look away, yet her brandy hued eyes mesmerized him. His heart did the same thing it had when she took his hand. He hated that he had no control over it.

Meg glanced back down at the baby breaking the hold she had on him. Confused by what had just happened, he walked away from her, trying to get rid of that unsettled feeling.

A huge commotion came from the back of the house and all the kids raced by them and headed out the front door.

Noah stopped when he saw Dix standing there.

"They are going up to the tree farm. Can I go?"

Dix glanced over at Meg. "Are they allowed up there?"

"Absolutely."

Dix nodded to Noah and he was gone in a flash.

If Meg hadn't known any better, she could've sworn she and Dix had a moment when he gazed into her eyes. But as fast as it happened it vanished making her think she might be crazy for even thinking such a thing. It would have been an understatement to say Dix acted standoffish. He might as well be wearing armor the way he deflected any kind of physical or emotional arrows being flung in his direction.

Colton had fallen back to sleep. "I'll be right back," she said.

Back in the dining room, she handed a sleeping Colton off to his father and returned to Dixon.

"Dessert will be served in about an hour and we have about that much time before it gets dark. You want to see what the kids are up to?"

He hesitated then nodded.

The temperature outside was about forty-five degrees, not bad for Thanksgiving Day in New England. The town of Chelsea wasn't too far from the Connecticut shoreline and every so often the breeze whipped, snapping the American flag in the front yard, making it seem colder.

"You never realize how much heat all those bodies throw off until you come outside," Meg said.

Dix looked like a turtle going back inside his shell the way he tucked his neck into his jacket. He kept his hands in his pockets as they walked side by side.

"It's cold," he murmured.

Meg smiled. "Are you kidding? This is nice. It's not cold until the temperatures get into the single digits."

Brody took off barking after the kids as they darted in and out from behind the blue spruces and fir trees near the Christmas Loft.

"Are the kids really okay up there?" he asked.

"As long as they don't take a saw and start cutting down trees, they're fine."

Dix shivered and Meg took pity on him. She pulled a set of keys from her jacket pocket, opened the Christmas Loft, and stepped inside. After turning on the lights, she went over to the propane fireplace. She flipped another switch and the hearth glowed red.

"It won't be long before the place heats up."

Dix nodded and looked over to where the decorated Christmas trees were on display. "No wonder my uncle asked you to decorate for him. You did all of this yourself?"

"Most of it. Gran helps sometimes. I'm going to put some water on. Would you like a cup of tea or hot chocolate?"

"Hot chocolate."

Pops had added the little kitchen in the back of the shop so they could offer customers a warm beverage while they shopped. Gran insisted on it, saying good hospitality is what people kept coming back for year after year. Meg agreed.

When she walked back into the shop, Dix stood directly in front of the fireplace. He'd dressed for dinner like he was going into the office with a button-down shirt, pants, leather shoes she assumed made by an Italian designer, and a casual jacket. Gran said he might need to be loved as much as his son did, but Meg doubted that. He made it clear he had no interest in finding anyone to help him put back the pieces of his broken heart.

"I was thinking about doing one of Jerry's trees in red and white, like this one," Meg said pointing to a six-foot fake fir tree that she'd decorated with white lights. Red and clear glass hearts along with red velvet bows were fastened to every bough while fluffy white garland entwined the branches.

Dix stood back and inspected it from every angle. "I don't know. Given Jerome's past, I'm not so sure he'd appreciate all the hearts."

Meg hadn't thought about that. Jerome's heart had been smashed, not just broken.

"You're right. Maybe this one?"

She pointed to the seven-foot blue spruce she'd decorated with silver and blue glass ornaments with silver garland. Meg always thought it had a masculine feel to it. The angel on top wore a flowing white and blue gown and glowed beautifully.

"Yes, he might like this."

Dix still didn't sound convinced but at least she'd engaged him in conversation, avoiding the awkward silence.

"I think I'll take pictures of all of these and show them to Jerry. Then he can make the choice himself," she said.

Meg went back to the counter to get her phone for the photos while Dixon strolled around the shop, weaving in and out between the trees.

"How do you decorate your tree back in California?" she asked, to keep the conversation going.

"I bought one of those trees that..." he looked around the shop. "Like that."

She followed Dix's gaze to the fiber optic tree that Gran insisted they stock especially for their older clientele. She said some people wanted a tree in the house but didn't want the bother of decorating. The trees were about two feet tall and had to put on a table if you wanted anyone to see it from the street. They served a purpose, but to Meg, they were garish and lacked a Christmas feel.

"So, Noah has never decorated a Christmas tree?" She couldn't even imagine that.

"He does at school."

Meg's heart squeezed in sympathy for the poor kid, thinking

of him alone at school. She wondered what happened to Noah's mother, but it seemed to be a sticky subject, so she wouldn't ask.

"You don't approve of that, either, do you?"

Meg laughed. "Again, none of my business."

"Well," Dix said, hesitating and rubbing the back of his neck, "seeing as though you're going to be spending a lot of time with us as you decorate the mansion, I'll share something personal."

"Dix, we barely know each other. If it makes you uncomfortable, don't. I understand."

He walked back to the counter where she stood. "Look, Meg, I'm not used to being part of a family that shares, but after sitting with yours at dinner, I can see the benefit of it. And I think if you're going to be with Noah for a couple of weeks you should know what happened to his mother. The last time I saw her seven years ago at court, she handed over all her parental rights to me, got her divorce, and left."

"Oh, Dix. I'm sorry," Meg said, exhaling like someone just sucker-punched her.

"It wasn't entirely her fault, though. When we found out she was pregnant, she wanted to, have the situation taken care of, and go our separate ways. I convinced her to have the baby and marry me."

Meg clenched her fists thinking about why Dix would have to convince the mother of his child to marry him but reminded herself she had promised she wouldn't ask so many questions.

Dixon had wandered over to the display of Christmas lights then came back over to the counter. "I was an idiot for thinking that once she had Noah, she'd stay. I learned a valuable lesson."

"What's that?"

"Money can't buy love."

"Well, duh."

That got a chuckle out of him, but Meg's heart weighed heavy in her chest. She lost her mother in a tragic accident. When she fell in love and the time came for her to have children of her own, she would make sure she was always there for them. She hated that their entire conversation had made her sick to her stomach.

The tea kettle whistled at the same time the kids shrieks could be heard off in the distance.

Meg ran into the kitchen area and poured the steaming water into the two mugs with the hot cocoa mix.

"When does Noah go back to school?" she asked, handing him his mug.

"After the New Year. We're leaving the day after the ball."

"Home to your fiber optic tree and warm California sunshine?"

"Exactly. I have a business to run."

"Oh, right. The real estate business."

"Jerome started it with my grandfather, his father. My Dad took it over but he and my mother recently retired."

Dix hardly sounded passionate about his life's work but at least there she got a clearer picture of his family and their dynamic.

"Where does that ladder go?" Dix nodded toward the back of the shop where a ladder leaned against the wall and disappeared into the ceiling.

She was usually better about putting away the ladder after she'd been up in the loft but totally forgot this morning.

"That's the loft."

"What's up there?"

Meg's cheeks heated. "It's storage for my supplies."

He eyed her more closely. "Why do I think you're not telling me the whole story?"

She'd been so used to keeping the loft her little secret. Gran knew, but that was it. Telling Dix probably wouldn't matter. He had no interest in her, and he had just shared something pretty personal of his own with her.

"It's my secret little nook. Kind of like a treehouse is to kids."

A warm smile spanned his face, and her cheeks heated.

"And why would you need that?"

"I love my family, but as you can see, I have a lot of cousins. Because I lived with Gran and Pops, whenever family members came to visit, I had to share everything. I used the loft to hide my favorite things so the others wouldn't play with them."

Her hot chocolate cooled off enough for her to take a sip without burning her mouth.

"What do you have up there?" Dix asked.

"A bed, my favorite blanket from when I was a kid, books I love. Stuff like that."

"I'd like to take a look sometime."

"Why?" She had to know why the stuffy, standoffish guy cared about her or her loft space.

"I'm in real estate. I'm curious."

"Okay, but another time. Right now, we should go back in before all the dessert is gone."

Chapter Five

Evie Darling gave Dix a huge box filled with plastic containers of various shapes and sizes, all with matching red lids. Inside each container was some part of the meal Dix and Noah shared with them.

She brought out a cookie tin and placed it in the box last.

"These are for Jerry. The Christmas we shared together before he went off to war, my mother made her famous minced meat squares. He raved about them in his letters that he sent home before he went missing in action." Evie's expression looked wistful as she recalled the memory. "Anyway, I'm sending them as a peace offering."

Dix smiled. "Do you want me to relay a message?"

"I do. Tell him Cliff and I are coming to his ball, and I'm expecting a dance."

"I'll tell him." Dix was never the hugging, kissing type. He grew up in a home where you didn't kiss your elders unless you were asked to but for the first time in his life it just seemed like kissing Evie was the right thing to do. He gave her a simple peck on the cheek. "Thank you for everything."

"It was our pleasure. You and Noah are welcome anytime."

Noah had no problem with the hugging and kissing. He hugged Evie and even shook Pops' hand.

Pops glanced over to Dix. "You're a single dad, huh?"

"I am."

Pops gave a curt nod. "Keep up the good work."

"Thank you, sir. I will."

They said goodbye to the rest of the crowd. Meg followed them out to the car.

"Ethan and Charlie said they're coming back tomorrow to help with the Christmas trees. Can I come too?" Noah asked Meg.

"I don't know, Bud. It's hard work. And you end up covered in dirt and tree sap. Are you up for that?"

"Yeah!"

Meg glanced over at him.

"It only took one day hanging out with my cousins for him to start speaking and acting like a normal kid," Meg said.

Dix had never seen Noah smile so much.

"Can I, Dad?"

"You sure you want him for the whole day?"

Meg put her arm around Noah. "He won't be any trouble. And if he is, I'll send him to the barn. Be here at six-thirty."

Dix's heart sank. "In the morning?"

"See you bright and early."

Back at the mansion, he found Jerome in front of the television and placed the tin from Evie in his lap.

"What's this?" he croaked.

"A gift from Evie Darling. Open it."

He lifted the lid and the pungent scent of cloves combined with spicy cinnamon filled the air.

"Is it... minced meat?" Jerome's voice cracked with emotion and tears pooled in his eyes when up looked up at Dix.

"She said it's one of your favorites."

Jerome nodded. He picked up one of the squares and took a bite.

"Is it as good as you remember?" Dix asked, sitting on the sofa next to him.

"It's better than I remember. How was it?" Jerome asked.

"If you're asking about dinner, it was delicious. If you want to know about Evie, she's still beautiful. Oh, and she told me to tell you that she'll be at the ball and wants you to save her a dance."

Jerome's eyes widened in surprise.

"I guess that means you should work on getting out of that chair." Dix never could figure the reason Jerome sat in the chair in the first place. He'd never fallen or broken any bones.

"Is she bringing that idiot husband of hers?"

"She is."

"Then I don't need to get out of this chair."

Dix rubbed a hand over his face. "Don't you want to feel her in your arms again?"

Jerome's eyes grew wider still at Dix's question. "I...well, I..."

"Look, Uncle, you told me to go to the Darlings, and I'm glad I did. We walked through the front door of that house a stranger and left feeling like family. You could use a couple of old friends. Get out of that chair and dance with Evie. You won't regret it."

Dixon left the room to go up to bed. Early the next morning, he woke to Noah tapping him on the shoulder.

"Dad, you awake?" Noah whispered.

Dix rubbed his eyes. "I am now."

"Megan said if I get there early enough, I can get the eggs from the chickens."

"I'll shower and meet you downstairs."

Twenty minutes later they were in the car headed back to the Darlings. The dawn started to give way to the daylight coming up over the tree farm. There was absolutely no traffic, something that never happened in LA.

As they drove down the driveway and pulled up near the house, Megan came out of the back door. Her hair was hidden under that beanie. She wore her work boots and a flannel jacket.

When she saw them, she waved, and he saw she had mittens on her hands.

Noah waved back. "There's Meg, Dad."

"I see her." Dix waved, too.

"Ethan told me yesterday that Megan was going to get married, but the guy broke her heart."

Dix put the car in park. He had no idea how reliable that kind of information was from a couple of nine-year-olds. "You mean he broke up with her."

"No. Meg was at the church ready to get married. The guy never came."

Dix's chest tightened when he pictured Meg standing in the back of a church in a white gown, waiting. Or up in her secret loft hiding place alone, sobbing.

Meg walked toward them wearing her constant smile.

Noah jumped out and ran to her. Dix followed along behind them. In the short time they'd met Meg, she managed to form a bond with Noah. A vision crossed Dix's mind of Noah coming home from school, while Meg met him at the door. He shook his head to get rid of such a crazy image then sprinted to catch up with them.

"Morning sunshine," Meg called over her shoulder hurrying down the little dirt path toward the chicken coop. They reached the fenced-in area together.

"Are you always this happy at the crack of dawn?" Dix asked.

Meg giggled. "Always."

"How do I do it, Meg?" Noah asked standing by the end of the coop that looked like a smaller version of the barn.

"Go inside the area where the coop is. Don't worry about the chickens. They'll move out of your way."

Noah opened the gate and tiptoed inside still holding the basket Megan gave him.

"Now what?"

"Open the side door on the house. If they laid any eggs, they should be right there."

Dix held his breath as Noah opened the door. The kid was going to be awfully disappointed if there was nothing in there.

"I see three!"

Meg clapped for him. "Gently pick them up and place them carefully in your basket. If you want, bring them into Gran so she can cook them for you."

"Awesome!"

Noah came out of the coop, closed the gate, and did a funny power walk back up the house so as not to break the eggs.

"I think you just made his day," Dix said.

"I'm glad. At least he sounds like a normal kid now. Oh, there's Matt." She waved at her cousin as he climbed out of his SUV.

"Glad to see Meg recruited you," Matt said shaking Dix's hand. "We could use all the help we can get with Pops not being able to pitch in this year."

Meg gave him a sheepish grin. "I didn't exactly ask you to help, but since you're here, would you mind?"

Dix had nothing else to do.

"Not at all."

"Great. Gran will make us breakfast before we go down to the barn."

"How far can three eggs go?"

"This time of year, we also get eggs from the market up the road."

Noah was just finishing up his eggs when the three of them paraded inside. The kitchen smelled like cinnamon again as Evie stood at the stove dropping donuts into boiling oil.

She told Meg to grab the bacon and scrambled eggs warming in the oven while Noah ran back outside to see Ethan and

were finished, Dix helped Meg carry three trays of nuts down to the little shed they sold the trees

in for hanging out to help," Meg said.

"It's my pleasure. I have to admit, I love watching Noah have such a good time."

Meg broke a donut in half and handed a piece to him. "And what about you? Are you having a good time?"

"It's odd. I really thought my entire time here I'd be holed up at the mansion. This is a pleasant surprise. What else do you do for fun around here, Meg?"

"I go out with my friends to the movies or dinner. Leia's been my best friend since middle school, so I hang out at her and Matt's house a lot."

Meg nibbled more on her half of the donut and he wondered if what Noah told him about being left at the altar was true. How could he ask her without sounding so presumptuous?

"Hey, Noah told me something this morning, and I was wondering if he got his information straight."

Meg picked her head up.

"Oh yeah? What did he tell you?"

"That you were left at the altar."

She tossed her head back and groaned. "I guess Ethan and Charlie were talking again, huh?"

"They told Noah."

"Yes, it's true," she said taking a deep breath and blowing it out.

"I'm sorry to hear that. I was hoping the kids were wrong."

"Nope, they weren't. It sucked, but I've moved on. I just attended a wedding of a mutual friend of ours. He was there with his plus one. I managed to get through the day without crying once, so yay me."

Dix fought the urge to give her a friendly comforting hug shocked that his usual standoffish behavior seemed to be almost non-existent around the Darlings. Or this particular Darling, anyway.

"I guess the next question is, does your grandfather have to beat the guys away from your door?"

"Ha! Not exactly. I'm too busy to date. I've come to t

with what happened. Things happen for a reason, right?" She had a bounce in her step on her way to the door.

"What do you think the reason is?"

She opened the door to the Christmas Loft wide and flipped the sign from closed to open before spinning back toward him. "He wasn't who I was meant to be with."

Chapter Six

The day after Thanksgiving had always been crazy busy and this year exceeded their expectations. Matt had gone up to close the gate while Meg cashed out the register. The door creaked open, and Dix stepped inside.

"I never knew how physically demanding it is to throw a tree through the netting machine and tie it onto someone's car."

Dix had a piece of fir tree stuck to his coat. Meg plucked it off.

"I'm sure you'll sleep like a baby tonight."

She turned to go back to the counter, and Dix grasped her hand. Heat shimmied up her arm as she glanced down at their entwined hands. She rather liked his touch, but raised her eyes to his, curious what he was thinking. He quickly let go.

"I don't know why I did that. Yes, I do. I'm having a great time, Meg. It's only five o'clock, and I don't want to go back to my uncle's mansion just yet."

She stared at him and his gaze never wavered. "What did you have in mind, Dix?" She lifted a questioning brow at him, while her pulse picked up speed.

"I thought if you were doing something exciting, I could...I mean we, Noah and me, could tag along?"

"I don't know if you'll be able to handle the excitement," she said, making sure her tone sounded heavy with sarcasm.

"Try me." His mouth curved into a slow, easy grin.

"I thought I could decorate one of the trees in Jerry's house like something from his childhood. To do that, tonight I have plans to make popcorn and string it together with cranberries. I know it sounds like something they only do in those cheesy Christmas movies, but I could really use the help. I also wouldn't blame you if you said no."

Dix's mouth relaxed making the area around his chocolate eyes soften. A far cry from the guy who just two days before made it very clear he had no interest in being near any woman.

"I think it sounds great."

Meg's heart skipped a beat. He sounded so flipping sincere, her insides warmed as if she'd just had a mug of Gran's hot mulled cider.

"Great. I just have to go up to the loft to get a few things. Want to help?"

Dix followed her to the back of the shop, and she climbed the ladder. Once in the loft, she headed to the left where she kept extra supplies for making ornaments and wreaths. While she tore the lid off one container, she heard Dix come up the ladder.

Meg grabbed an empty plastic container that she used to cart items up and down. She tossed in two balls of white string, several different colored spools of ribbon along with two big paper sacks of pinecones she'd collected on the farm. When she packed all the things she needed to make decorations for Jerry's tree, she straightened from her crouched position to see Dix looking at her small bookcase.

"This place is amazing, Meg. I expected to see some dirty, dusty crawl space. This is more like an apartment."

"Yeah. I used to spend a lot of time up here."

She sat on the twin mattress she'd covered with the quilt Gran made her when she was a little girl.

"You're beautiful, just like your mom," Dix said picking up the framed photo of her parents.

"Thanks, Dix." Her cheeks heated from his compliment. She'd always thought her mother was beautiful, with her dark hair and doe-like eyes.

He replaced the picture and sat next to her on the bed.

"You're more than looks, though, Meg. You're so real. I haven't found that in women back in LA."

Her face suddenly felt hot again, and it wasn't from heat rising to the loft from the propane fireplace.

"Wow, Dix, are you always that honest?"

He laughed. "I think you have something to do with that. I haven't told you this, but I've been thinking about leaving California to live here with my uncle."

Dix's shoulder brushed against hers, causing her blood to heat other parts of her body, a foreign sensation since before her wedding to Josh.

"What about Noah's boarding school?"

"I've been thinking hard about withdrawing him. My uncle keeps saying to let him just be a kid. And after spending time with your family, I think I'm missing out on being a good dad, you know?"

Dix leaned back on his elbows and stretched his legs out. He smelled like spruce and pine, which she loved. His scent made it hard for her not to lean into him, making her realize she really needed to start dating again.

"You're the only family he has, Dix. It makes total sense."

Dix grasped her hand in his. This time when she glanced up into his eyes, he didn't let go. When he brought her hand up to his lips, a shudder went through her as he affectionately kissed her knuckles.

"Dix, I've enjoyed this past couple of days, but I'm sure part of what you're feeling is because of the holidays. Everyone gets more sentimental this time of year."

Dix interwove his fingers with hers.

"Are you always this rational or are you just doing it to protect your heart, Meg?"

"Both."

His deep laugh made her grin.

"That's funny," he said. "I've always kept my guard up, too, never sharing with women I've dated. I don't seem to be having that problem with you."

Meg knew exactly what he meant. As hokey as it sounded, being with Dix, the pieces of her heart seemed to be put back together. But, as he said, she was sensible. She had a good head on her shoulders and to dream about love and a life together with someone she'd only just met was ridiculous and it would be pointless.

"We've only known each other for a few days."

Dix would be leaving Chelsea the day after the ball and she'd never see or hear from him again. He could say all he wanted about choosing to live here instead of LA, but Meg was sure once he returned home, he'd realize what a mistake he was making and decide to stay there.

The right thing for her to do would be to keep things light-hearted between them. That way, no one got hurt.

"Meg!" Matt shouted from below.

"Up here!" She called back.

Meg attempted to stand but Dix pulled her back down.

Before she could stop him, his soft lips were on hers. She put her hand on his chest to give him a gentle push back until Dix cradled her cheeks in his hands so gently, she stopped fighting and melted into him. Her body heated as he deepened their kiss.

He withdrew away from her first, leaving her shaken to her core.

Meg jumped up and ran over to the containers without looking back at him. Her heart pounded in her ears and when she slapped her hands to her cheeks, they were hot.

"I uh, I needed some things for decorating Jerome Graham's Christmas tree." She hollered down to her cousin. "Dix is helping me."

She gave the box a hard shove with her foot and it skidded to a stop right in front of Dixon. His mouth broke into a grin when he waved down to Matt.

Matt nodded and gave them both a knowing grin. "Decorating the tree, huh? Is that what the kids are calling it these days?"

Meg's cheeks continued to burn as Dix climbed down the ladder a few rungs then lifted his arms for the box, looking very pleased with what they'd just shared.

Dix sat in the Darling's kitchen surrounded by huge bowls of popcorn and fresh cranberries while Noah helped Gran make popcorn balls to give to customers along with her cider donuts and hot chocolate.

As he strung another cranberry with the huge darning needle, he thought about kissing Meg in the loft. Even her kisses were honest. He wondered what would happen if he did live there. They could try to have a real relationship. Would she give him all her heart and not hold back? Is that even what he wanted? It had been so long since he'd been with anyone, his heart was hard as a rock.

Meg sat across from him at the table and sang along to the Carpenter's song, Merry Christmas, Darling. Her singing voice was a sweet as the rest of her.

She looked up from her strand of popcorn and cranberries and caught him staring at her. "How's it going over there?" Meg quirked an eyebrow at him and gave him a lopsided smirk.

"Good." He lifted his own strand to show her. "What do you think?"

"It looks great. But here's a word of advice—keep your eyes on your work. I wouldn't want you to get stuck with that needle. Blood doesn't look all that festive on the popcorn."

Dix chuckled. "If I do, it would be your fault."

"My fault? How do you figure that?"

"I'm having a hard time keeping my eyes off you."

Meg groaned. "Do you use that lame line on all the girls?"

"Not in a very long time."

Meg popped a piece of popcorn into her mouth. "You know, seeing as though neither one of us has dated in a while, maybe we could dip our toes back into the dating game by going out with each other."

"How would that work?" He hadn't meant his tone to sound so skeptical, because the idea intrigued him. He put down his needle.

"It would be like a holiday fling. Have a few dates, have a lot of fun, and after the ball is over, so are we. We go into it with eyes wide open, no expectations, yet we're back in the dating game. Kind of like a pitcher warming up in the bullpen before going into the big game."

"I love a good baseball analogy."

"So, you like the idea?" she asked.

His heart accelerated as Megan stabbed another cranberry and threaded it down to the piece of popcorn.

"I do."

"Good. Where do you want to go on our first date?"

"You're more familiar with the area. You pick."

A short time later, Gran pulled out the leftover turkey and all the fixings for sandwiches so Noah wouldn't eat only popcorn balls for dinner.

"I'll go get Pops," Noah said running into the living room after Gran and Meg set the table.

Megan glanced over at Dix. "I love that kid."

Dix nodded. "He's going to help your grandfather because he

told me earlier that he loves that you all eat together at the table and talk."

"Aww... that's cute."

"I think he's got a crush on you, Meg," Gran said, placing the gravy boat on the table.

"I know I do," Dix said.

Meg's cheeks pinked up with embarrassment as she threw a potholder at him. "Stop that."

After dinner, they finished up the popcorn and cranberry garland then progressed to making red and green construction paper chains. Dix's fingers were still stained red from the cranberries, but he didn't care. If someone told him a month ago that he'd be having a great time making old-fashioned Christmas decorations, he never would've believed them. But sitting there with Meg doing just that made him feel like a weight had been lifted off him. And he hadn't felt like that in forever.

"I don't know about you, Dix, but I'm exhausted," Meg said an hour later.

"I'm getting there. I think Noah crashed on the sofa an hour ago."

"We got pretty far. Tomorrow I'll cut the trees for Jerry's house then on Sunday I'll start decorating."

Dix helped her clean up and put the boxes in the pantry. He stood in the doorway blocking her way.

"Excuse me," she said.

He looked down at her. Their gazes met, and her eyes sparkled with humor.

"So, does the fling mean we can kiss more?" He teased.

Every time he thought about their kiss his blood caught fire. His whole life he'd been with women who wanted things from him, material things, like jewelry, houses, or money. Not his love, and definitely not his friendship.

With Meg standing near him smelling like pine trees and popcorn, he felt... safe. It sounded ridiculous, even to him. But as far he could tell, Meg didn't have some underlying ulterior motive. They'd only known each other for a few days, but she had been through something similar. Her heart had been smashed into pieces.

His question still hung in the air between them. What the hell was he thinking? He couldn't believe the words that had just tumbled from his lips.

She hadn't taken her eyes off of him, making his heart race with panic.

"Well," she said, her voice just above a whisper, "the word 'fling' insinuates more than just kissing, doesn't it?"

He swallowed. "It could. If that's what we're agreeing to."

She licked her lips and nodded. "Maybe we could play that part by ear. Sometimes feelings get in the way, and I don't want this to get messy."

"I do have to go back home and settle things there to make a permanent move here, but I plan on coming back, Meg."

"Let's leave that part out of it, Dix. We both know things could change and you might not come back."

He totally understood where she came from now. She wouldn't allow herself to get hurt again. He might not want just a fling with her, but they would cross that bridge when they got there.

"Should we shake on it?" She held her hand out to him.

He shook her hand then brought it up to his lips and kissed it. "It's a deal."

"Thanks for all your help today."

"You're welcome."

He got on his coat while Meg gently woke Noah. She walked out with them to the car and helped his very sleepy son get in. After Dix closed the door, Meg leaned up against the car and suddenly just a word of goodbye didn't seem like enough.

Dix cupped her cheek in his hand and lowered his mouth to hers to give her a slow, sweet goodbye kiss. But Meg wrapped her arms around his neck and responded to him so deeply and passionately the cold air around them sizzled with heat. It took all his strength to pull back away from her to leave for home.

"When I see you tomorrow, we'll talk about where you want to go on our first date," he whispered against her lips. "Goodnight, Meg."

"'Nite, Dix."

Chapter Seven

Between Dix's scorching hot kiss and their 'deal,' Meg had a hard time falling asleep. She loved the idea of getting back into dating by dating each other. He played it off like he would be back after he left for California, but she wouldn't hold him to it. He had responsibilities with his business, she understood that. She'd look at this little fling as a Christmas present to herself. She'd been hurt so badly. If going out with Dix helped to ease the pain from Josh's betrayal, even for the few weeks, it would be worth it.

Even though she hadn't fallen asleep until well after midnight, she and Brody went out at the first light of dawn. It smelled piney like Christmas trees and the nip in the air made everything fresh. She'd tagged the trees she wanted for Jerry's mansion and cut them down before the rush of customers.

She chopped down the White Fir and dragged it to the trailer attached to the tractor, then drove to where she tagged the Balsam. She sawed the trunk then shoved that one next to the White Fir onto the trailer, too. Brody came running when she whistled and the two of them drove back down the hill.

As she steered around the barn to the Christmas Loft, her heart tripped seeing Dix as he waved at her. Memories of their goodnight kiss came flooding back, and even in the brisk wind, those thoughts warmed her. Meg ground her teeth together to steel herself against the rush of emotion that rose within her. A fun fling was one thing, but she couldn't fall for him. Her heart wouldn't be able to handle it when it came time for him and Noah to leave.

"You look beautiful up there," Dix said as he gave her his hand and helped her climb down from the tractor.

"Thank you, but really, you need to stop. I won't be able to get my beanie on with my head so big."

He lowered his head and she met his lips with hers. Because even with all her talk of not falling for him, she couldn't resist his kisses and what they did to her. Dix made her feel wanted, and it had been over a year since Josh abandoned her, for the second time in her life, though her parents certainly didn't do it on purpose.

"What a great way to start the day," he said when they parted.

"Agreed," she said, looking around behind him. "Where's Noah?"

"He went to see if there are any eggs." Dix pointed to the trailer. "I see you've been busy."

"Those are two of Jerry's trees. He wanted one for the foyer, too, but I haven't tagged that one yet."

Dix took her hand in his and together they walked back to the house for breakfast. They worked side by side for most of the day and genuinely enjoyed each other's company.

Before dusk settled in, Matt and Dix loaded up Jerome's trees into the pick-up truck, while Meg packed the decorations in the back of the double cab.

"Can I ride with you, Meg?" Noah asked.

"Sure, Bud, but I have to warn you. You'll have to hear Christmas music."

Noah shrugged and ran to climb up into the passenger seat.

"See you up there," she called to Dix.

Meg drove up the circular driveway and parked in front of the mansion. Between Dixon, Ramsey the butler, and a few guys from the kitchen, they brought in the trees. They put them in their prospective rooms and helped Dix put them in their stands. The housekeeper filled the stands with water.

They all stood back to admire the White Fir when Meg heard the robotic sound of Jerome's motorized scooter.

"What do you think?" Meg stepped back and held out her arms like Vanna White introducing the next puzzle on Wheel of Fortune.

If Meg didn't know any better, she could've sworn she saw tears in his eyes.

"Who picked that one?" Jerry asked.

"I did." Meg held her breath waiting to hear what Jerry would say next.

He gave her a curt nod. "It's a beauty."

She released her breath and smiled. "I'm so glad you approve. Would you like to see the other one?"

Jerry smiled. "Lead the way, Meg."

The first day Meg met with Jerry, he'd decided that the dancing portion of the Christmas ball should be held in the music room. Jerome said he'd have his staff move the beautiful grand piano to the formal living room the night of the party. There were windows from floor to ceiling that overlooked the formal gardens and would be a perfect spot for the Christmas tree. She had chosen the White Fir for its citrusy aroma and soft silvery needles and would decorate it with all white lights. Silver bows would be fastened to the branches while silver tinsel draped over the boughs to remind Jerry of Christmases past. Blue and white globe ornaments would be hung in between to complete it.

For the Christmas tree reminding Jerome of his childhood, Meg chose a Balsam Fir. Balsam Firs were the trees everyone had in the 30's and 40's. They were what reminded everyone of an 'old-fashioned' tree, with its medium, close together needles and smelled the most like a Christmas tree should.

His reaction to the Balsam was just a visceral and Meg didn't know whether to laugh or cry.

"Just wait until they're both all decorated," Meg said.

"Meg said we're all going to help, even you, Uncle Jerome."

Noah couldn't contain his excitement, but Jerry looked a little less than thrilled. His hopeful expression had gone back to a scowl, but Meg didn't want to upset the guy.

She tried to think of something to say but had nothing. Glancing over to Dix for help, he gave her a knowing nod. Dix placed his hand on Noah's shoulder. "Why don't you get washed up for dinner, Noah?"

The kid left the room as his father asked.

"I hired you, Meg, to decorate the trees," Jerome said softly.

"That's true, but Noah wanted to help. I might've mentioned something about how decorating the tree is a family tradition. Noah told me that you are part of his family," she said.

Dix's eyes locked on hers as she jerked her head in Jerome's direction silently asking for a little help with his grumpy uncle.

"You certainly aren't expected to help, Uncle. We know how much you hate it. We offered to help Meg because it's only two weeks before the ball. It's a lot for her to do alone."

Jerome accelerated his scooter across the floor to the door. "I'll leave you to it, then." He spun the chair around to leave then backed it up. "Dinner will be in five minutes. I'll expect you to be there, Meg."

The scooter made the robot sound as Jerome hit the button to accelerate again.

Meg turned to Dix. "He's so demanding. No wonder he's been single all these years."

Dix grinned. "I think it's his feeble attempt at match-making."

"Well, maybe you should tell him we're not interested in making a love match."

Meg left for the foyer with Dix on her heels.

"Meg, wait. Where are you going?"

"Since I've been forced to stay for dinner, I'll get the rest of the decorations out of the truck."

For the next week, Dix and Meg spent a good part of every day at the mansion. Between Dixon, Noah, and Meg, they decorated all the trees and all the rooms downstairs. Meg found the perfect tree for the foyer. Dix couldn't remember what kind it was, he just knew it was almost seven feet tall and it took all the manpower in the house to get it up and in the tree stand.

When Meg left each night, the mood of the mansion became deflated, especially Dix's. Then his heart pounded in excitement when she walked through the front doors each morning. She insisted they play Christmas music, and Dix noticed that even Jerome's staff acted differently with Meg around. They didn't walk around with pinched faces and smiled a hell of a lot more.

But his favorite part of each day was when they finished up the decorating and he and Meg would put Noah to bed, then go out on a date.

They went to the movies, to a pizzeria for a famous New Haven-style pizza, the local cafe for coffee and dessert, and took a stroll around the town. One night, Meg hooked up Sam and Dean to the sleigh and they went on a joyride through the woods around the farm.

Meg placed a fleece blanket across their laps and the light of the full moon made the snow glisten. After going around the trail twice, they stopped to have the hot chocolate Evie had poured into a thermos for them.

"You never cease to amaze me," Dix said, sipping his drink with his arm around Meg as she leaned against him.

"What do you mean?"

"I mean, is there anything you can't do?"

"Oh, there's plenty, trust me."

He kissed the top of her head. "I don't believe you."

"You don't know me that well."

"I haven't known you that long, but from what I do know, you are kind and trustworthy. Let's not forget you singlehandedly cured my uncle's depression."

Meg finished her hot chocolate then sat up and kissed him. It started off with just their lips lightly brushing against each other until she playfully introduced her tongue to his. The blanket slid down on the floor, not that they needed it anyway with kisses like that.

"Meg, we should stop. I don't want to, uh, go to the next level out here."

"Come on, Dix. Where's your sense of adventure?"

"It's in the warmth of my bedroom back at the mansion, where I can undress you slowly. You deserve more than a quickie in a cramped sleigh in freezing temperatures."

He purposely kept his penetrating gaze on hers, so she'd know he meant every word.

"Damn you, Dix. How is this thing between us supposed to be a fling, if you're getting all emotional and mushy on me?"

She put the cap back on the thermos and put the mugs in the basket, before placing the blanket back on their laps and grabbing the reins.

"Okay, you win this one," she said, smiling. "But only because I think you deserve the same."

At the beginning of the second week, Jerome made an appearance as they were putting the finishing touches on the ballroom.

"There he is," Meg called out to him. "The host with the most...or something like that."

Noah busted out laughing, which made him laugh, too. He appreciated her easy-going manner.

Nothing ruffled her, not even Jerome and his nit pickiness, especially when his uncle criticized how she decorated the tree that reminded him of his childhood.

"You skimped on the tinsel," he barked.

Meg stood back with her hand on her hips and stared at the tree for a few minutes.

"It does look a little bare in spots," she admitted.

Meg grabbed another box of tinsel and strolled over to Jerome. "Here you go. Have at it."

"What?" His uncle wrinkled up his face in a glower.

"Fill in the empty spots."

Jerome frowned. "I can't do it from down here. It needs more tinsel near the top."

"Ohh. Okay."

Meg motioned for Dix to help her lift Jerome out of the chair. When Jerome realized what they were doing, he started batting at them as if they were pesky flies.

"Get away from me. You know I can't stand up."

Meg stood back. "My grandmother wants a dance with you, so no time like the present to practice getting up and down out of that thing."

Jerome crossed his arms over his chest and pouted like a spoiled child.

"Come on, Jerry. You promised. And Dix told me that your word is the one thing people can count on around here."

Silence fell over the room. A few minutes passed, and Dix shook his head. Jerome did whatever Jerome wanted, whenever he wanted. Meg would lose this battle.

Dix rubbed his eyes. When he opened them, Jerome had placed his hands on the arms of the chair and attempted to push himself up.

"That's it, Jerry." Meg put her arm around his back. Dix hurried over to help him stand the rest of the way.

Jerome wobbled a little on his feet, but he stood.

"We're right here, Jerry. We won't let you fall." Meg encouraged him to keep standing.

After a few minutes, he made Meg take her hands away, but Dix kept one arm around Jerome's waist.

"Give me that damn tinsel," Jerome said through gritted teeth.

Megan gave him a handful. Jerome raised his arms and began draping it over some of the higher branches.

"Now that's how it's done," he said.

Jerome stayed standing for ten minutes before he sat in his chair again.

Each day after that, Meg and Dix would help him stand for long stretches of time. Two days before the ball, Meg called him into the music room.

"Come on, Jerry. Doris Day is singing The Christmas Waltz, and I want to see your rad dance moves."

She placed her iPhone on the side table, and it sounded like an orchestra invaded the room. Horns and violins played the 50's classic.

His uncle smiled, a real, genuine smile, melting Dix's heart.

"Help me up, Dixon," Jerome ordered.

He didn't have to help too much. Jerome had regained some strength in his legs over the past week. But would he be able to dance?

Meg put her hand in his hand and the other on his shoulder while Jerome placed a hand on her waist. They started off shaky, but by the middle of the song when the music changed to your typical waltz timing, Jerome glided over the newly waxed floor with Meg in his arms.

They had been working outside earlier that morning, wrapping white twinkle lights around the trees in the front yard when Noah had started a snowball fight. Because their coats, hat, and boots were wet, they'd taken them off in the mudroom off the kitchen. Consequently, they were all in stocking feet, and Meg's hair wasn't pushed up inside her beanie. It had loosened from her ponytail, but she was in the most natural state and never looked more beautiful than she did just then in Jerome's arms.

The song ended and Dix worried for Jerome who panted to catch his breath. He ran over and jumped in the motorized chair speeding over to his uncle.

"Here, sit."

Jerome reluctantly sat down while laughing the entire time.

"You can tell Evie I'll be waiting for that dance."

Meg beamed and her eyes shimmered with tears. "I will."

Jerome turned his scooter and headed for the door, while Meg's phone had gone onto another Christmas song. She went over to stop it.

"Don't turn it off, Meg," Dix stopped her. "Play the waltz again."

"Why?" She drew her eyebrows together, confused by his request.

"May I have this dance?" Dix bowed in front of her.

"Seriously? You know how to waltz?"

"My mother had dreams of me attending a few debutante balls to meet a girl in high society, so she made me take ballroom dance lessons when I was a teenager."

Meg hit the screen on her phone and the strains of the waltz played from the speakers once again.

He took her in his arms and gazed into her eyes. "We've been so busy this week, we've hardly been alone."

"I know, right? I miss our make-out sessions," she said still a little out of breath from her dance with his uncle.

Dix moved her across the floor thrilled to be standing close and impressed at how well she followed his lead. Her eyes never left him, and his heart nearly exploded seeing the integrity there. When the song wound down, Dix spun her around, whirled her back toward him, and dipped her in his arms. He ended by kissing her firmly on the mouth. When he drew back, her cheeks flushed.

"It's a good thing we're not alone in the house right now, Megan Darling," he said in a low tone. "I would kiss you like you deserve to be kissed, and you'd become putty in my hands."

"Don't let me stop you," Jerome said matter-of-factly.

"Jerry!" Meg half-laughed, half-reprimanded him. "I thought you left."

"I was going to, but I wanted to see how well Dix's dance

lessons paid off. I'm glad I stuck around. You're good for him, Meg. Dixon, don't be an idiot and let her get away."

Meg grinned still holding the dipping position. "Well, at least there's nothing wrong with your hearing, Jerry."

Even Jerome laughed before he finally left the room, and Dix set Meg back on her feet.

"Your cheeks are still very pink," he said smiling.

"I'm just wondering what becoming putty in your hands would feel like."

He took a step closer to her. "You could stay and find out."

"And get to experience the adventure of the warmth of your bedroom?"

"Exactly." He followed Meg over to the table where she had her iPhone, which played "White Christmas."

"These past three weeks with you Meg, made me realize something about you."

"Oh yeah?"

"You put your entire soul into everything you do. I've watched you with Noah, and I see it when you're with your family. Hell, you even love Jerome. That's a gift, Meg."

He closed the gap between them and grasped her hands in his. "I'm having deeper feelings for you, and to be honest, they're taking me completely by surprise. And unless I'm totally insane, I think you share those same feelings for me, too."

Meg put her arms around his neck. "I do, but unlike you, Dix, I push them away. You're leaving in a few days. I don't want to think about what could or couldn't happen after that. Can't we just enjoy what we have right now?"

Dix saw the hurt lurking behind her amber eyes. "I understand why you want to keep your heart locked up, but once I come back, you won't have to."

Meg sighed and muttered something about finishing the decorations. Dix let her go off alone. He wanted what he said to sink in. He wanted her to know how serious he was about him falling for her.

A little while later, Meg came into the music room.

"That should do it. I won't return until the night of the ball because I've got to catch up with some things at the farm."

She locked her hands lightly around his neck again and stood on her toes. She kissed his lips, gently at first. When he responded, she deepened it with her velvety tongue making his blood heat and causing a firestorm in his groin. He always let her take the lead, not wanting to rush her. He wanted her badly, but she would have to make the decision whether or not they would consummate their relationship.

He kissed her again. And again, her response made his blood catch fire.

Meg drew back, and in a whisper said, "What would you say if I told you I think I'd like to be putty now."

His heart kicked. "I'd say you don't have to tell me twice." Dix took her hand in his and led her to the large staircase up to his bedroom.

Chapter Eight

Dix gently closed the door behind them as Meg glanced around his bedroom. It was decorated for a man, with neutral tones and dark wood accents. Even the bed's headboard and footboard were deep mahogany.

But she hadn't come to Dix's bedroom to admire Jerome Graham's interior decorating skills. She did need a moment to compose herself, though. Her heart pounded, a mix of anxiety and excitement. She'd never just 'hopped into bed' with a guy, as Gran would say. She'd been with Josh for almost a year before they slept together. It was the same with her other exes. Meg just wasn't a casual sex kind of girl.

And that's why she thought of the fling thing. She and Dix certainly had chemistry. That had been obvious the second he kissed her in the loft, so, they'd probably be compatible in the bedroom. But even if they weren't, there'd be no harm, no foul. That's what a fling was for. There were no expectations. Just flirting and fun and the day after the ball, they'd move on with their lives.

That's what she told herself anyway. Truth be told, she couldn't be sure that after she and Dix were intimate that she wouldn't become an emotional mess when he did have to leave. It was new territory for her, and she'd just have to see what happened.

Dix leaned against the dresser. He'd pushed up the sleeves of his navy-blue polo shirt to his elbows like he was ready to get down to business. Doing so, revealed his Rolex and for some reason, her hormones thought it was the sexiest thing she'd ever seen, and they kicked into overdrive. The dark hair on his arms matched the hair on his head and his beard and she imagined his chest would be covered in it too. Her breath hitched and her pulse quickened thinking she would find that out very soon.

"It's going to be difficult for me to become putty with you way over there," she said, sitting on the bed.

"I was just giving you a chance to change your mind."

"Is that what you were hoping for?"

"Not at all. I just want to make sure that it's what you want."

"It is."

He gave a curt nod and in one fluid motion, he dragged his shirt up over his head, tossing it onto the top of the dresser. She sucked in a breath as he stalked toward her. Thick brown hair covered his broad chest and his lean abs weren't bad either.

He reached down, took his hand in hers, and pulled her up. Slowly he lowered his mouth to hers in a light kiss on the lips. She took the liberty to run her hands up and down his naked back as he continued his sensual onslaught of her mouth. He always left it to her to deepen their kisses, but this time when she attempted it, he drew away from her.

"Let's level the playing field," he said in a seductive tone.

"What do you have in mind?"

"This," he said as he undid the top button of her flannel shirt. He took his time working the buttons until he undid them all, keeping the promise he made on their sleigh ride that night by slowly pushing it off her. It only took one flick of his fingers to unclasp her bra but again, he made purposeful movements to remove it, until she stood in front of him shirtless, braless, and vulnerable.

"You're beautiful, Meg."

His mouth came crashing down on hers in an urgent, fiery kiss, leaving behind their sweet, sensual smooches.

He backed away from her, and she hated him for it, until she realized what he was doing, then followed suit. Pants and underwear flew off, neither one of them caring where they landed. Slow and steady might win a race, but fast and furious got the job done when it came to becoming completely naked.

He came back to her then, pulling her against him in another demanding kiss. Her nipples, already sensitive, tightened when they brushed up against the soft curls of his chest. While they kissed, he turned down the comforter on the bed behind her then tenderly laid her down into it. He managed to never break away from her lips as he lay next to her. He rolled on top of her, shifting his weight onto his arms so he wouldn't crush her.

He brushed his lips along her throat and down to her breast, dropping tiny kisses along the way until his hot tongue landed on her areola. She hissed in a breath and he grasped her hand and twined his fingers in hers. With his other hand, he caressed her right breast and the second his thumb grazed her hardness there, fire shot through her, landing on the most sensitive spot between her thighs.

He let go of her hand, stopped his sensuous assault, and rose above her, glancing down.

She blew out a breath, almost grateful for the break from the overload of pleasure.

"I am interrupting this regularly scheduled program in the name of safe sex."

She laughed as Dix reached over to the night table and pulled a condom from the drawer.

"You thought of everything. I wasn't worried about pregnancy because I have a thing."

He tore open the package. "A thing?"

"An IUD. But it was stupid of me to not think about condoms. I guess I'm out of practice."

"When you mentioned having a fling, I knew it didn't have to mean being intimate, but I thought it would be better to be prepared, just in case."

He rolled the condom down the length of him, grunting in his low tone as he reached the base. Heat consumed her, knowing it was a preview of what was to come.

He positioned himself over her and she lifted her hips. He slipped his arm under her waist to steady himself, and he entered her as gently as he could.

"I'm fine, Dix," she whispered, "Please, I really need..."

Without saying another word, he buried himself completely inside her and the both cried out.

"Is something wrong?" she asked, as he lay completed still.

Panic gripped her. Dix was a tall guy so his head was over her shoulder and she couldn't see his face to know if he was enjoying it or not.

"Not at all," he answered, his voice raspy with emotion. "I just wanted to give you a chance to, um, adjust to me."

Her heart melted and she sighed. "I'm good. Thanks for that, though."

The second she said it he began their rhythm. She met each thrust, her body demanding more, then more, then much more.

She needed to be touched everywhere, so she lifted her arms over her head. Dix willingly accepted and lowered his mouth to her erect peak. He nipped and licked her all while keeping their pace. When he sucked her nipple into his hot mouth, her body exploded in a mind-blowing orgasm.

"Fuck, don't stop," she cried, her body shuddering and shaking as he kept their frenetic pace. His mouth never left her breast until she was spent and said, "Okay, ohmigod," she panted.

Dix lifted his mouth away from her breast but kept his momentum. He held her tighter to him and groaned in her ear, thrusting faster and harder. She responded to him, still coming down from her own high when he released a moan. It had to be the hottest thing she ever heard.

He collapsed on top of her, both lying still for a little while to catch their breath.

He kissed her. "I'll be right back."

He left her for the bathroom, and she dug herself deeper under the sheets and down comforter, feeling replete.

Dix did everything right. Gentle when he needed to be, but when she needed more, he did that too. He'd been the perfect choice for a fling. Now if she could just convince her heart of that, everything would work out fine.

Dix came back into the bedroom. Meg had burrowed so deep under the down comforter that all he could see was the top of her head. He went around the bed and crawled in next to her.

"If you're cold, I'll turn up the heat," he said softly.

"I've never been this warm in my life, Dix. Thank you."

She moved over and laid her arm over his abdomen and her head on his chest. Cuddling. He'd missed that part of lovemaking, too.

He knew they'd be perfectly matched inside the bedroom, just by the way she kissed him.

They fell asleep in each other's arms. He didn't know how long they'd been asleep when he stirred because she moved away from him. He dozed off again only to be awakened at the sound of her moving around the room.

"Meg?" he called out as he flipped on the light on the bedside table.

"Oh. Hi."

She stood there completely dressed.

"Were you going to leave without saying goodbye?" His chest ached at the thought.

"No. I don't know, maybe."

He threw back the bed covers and stood in front of her wearing nothing but his boxer briefs.

"Talk to me, Meg."

"I should get back to the farm before Gran..."

Her voice trailed away, but Dix knew what she tried to say.

"Before they realize you never came home."

"Exactly," she looked relieved.

"You're a grown woman, Meg. I'm sure they know what's going on between us, and they'd understand if you spent the night with me."

"I'm not so sure about that, Dix."

"I just don't get why you wouldn't wake me to say goodbye."

Her sheepish expression before looking down at the floor made his gut twist.

"Do you regret what we did?"

Her head snapped up. "No, absolutely not. It was amazing." Meg, never at a loss for words, seemed to be struggling with what to say next.

"I just need some time, Dix." When her eyes met his they swam with tears.

"Did I say or do something wrong?"

Her tears spilled onto her cheeks and he gulped. He hated seeing her hurt like that and couldn't imagine what he'd done.

"No. You did everything right," she said half-laughing, half-crying. "That's part of the problem. When I was stupid enough to suggest this fling thing, I forgot something really important."

"What?"

"My heart."

"Your heart," he nodded, knowing where she was going with this.

"In my head, a Christmas romance sounded perfect. We'd have some fun then we'd fool around then both go our separate ways. But my dumb heart is saying, 'hey, what about me? This guy is great, and I'm falling for him.'"

She sniffed and wiped her wet cheeks. "See what I mean?"

"I do."

"I was an idiot to think I wouldn't get emotionally involved, especially once we," her gaze landed on his underwear then she jerked her head toward the bed, "once we had incredible sex."

"I'm going to let you in on a little secret. I've been emotionally involved since the night I kissed you in the loft on your childhood bed, Meg. It's why I'm coming back after Christmas."

She shook her head slowly. "I'm not naïve enough to believe promises like that, Dix. Things happen in life and people change."

"And I get that. You got burned by someone who made the biggest promise to you that anyone could ever make. But I'm not that guy. Coming to Chelsea has changed me, Meg. You have changed me. I will be back."

He closed the gap between them, placed his hand around the back of her neck, and pressed his mouth to hers. Her body immediately softened to his touch, and she kissed him back with the same hunger she had earlier in his bed.

He kissed her like that until he left her breathless.

"Take all the time you need, Meg. I'll be here when you're ready."

She left out the door and Dix silently hoped that wouldn't take too long.

Chapter Nine

Meg opted to wear a green velvet gown with a high neck and cap sleeves instead of the traditional red. She piled her hair upon her head and curled the pieces around her face. Gran let her borrow a white fake fur wrap to wear over it.

She'd been busy the past two days with farm stuff and Christmas things but that didn't mean she hadn't thought about Dix and the intimate time they shared. Those thoughts invaded her mind more than she wanted them to, and she blushed every time.

He had checked in with her via text, worried that he hadn't heard from her. She acknowledged him, saying she was fine, but couldn't ignore her family's business, and she'd see him at the ball. Nervous butterflies flitted in her stomach as she descended the stairs ready to go to the ball. She couldn't wait to see him again and hoped things wouldn't be weird between them.

"You look wonderful, Meg," Pops said.

Meg kissed his cheek and straightened his tie. "You look pretty dapper, yourself."

Gran came out of her bedroom wearing a silver beaded gown with silver slippers and carried a black and gray stole over her arm.

She spun around once. "How do I look?"

"Gorgeous, Gran."

Pops hobbled over to her and kissed her cheek. "As beautiful as our wedding day, Evie. That bastard, Graham, better keep his hands to himself."

Meg fastened the fur jacket and took the keys to the car from her clutch when the doorbell rang.

"Oh, Meg, would you get that?" Gran asked, now toying with her hair in front of the mirror in the hall.

Meg pulled open the door and her heart stumbled.

Dixon wore a wide smile standing there in a black tuxedo with a crisp white shirt. On one hand, he held a see-through plastic box holding a corsage. His other hand held a square black velvet jewelry box.

Her body thrummed at the sight of him.

"What are you doing here, Dix?"

"I meant to ask you to be my date to the ball, but we got caught up in other things and then you left."

Her cheeks heated in embarrassment recalling their last conversation.

"I'm sorry about leaving like that."

"I said I'll wait, and I will, as long as your heart is still saying the same thing."

She smiled. He really had listened to everything she said. "It is."

"Do you think you could say yes to be my date tonight?"

"I would love to be your date."

"What, are we heating the outside now?" Pops hollered. "Let the man inside, Meg."

Dix stepped inside. "You're beautiful, Meg."

Her insides turned to mush remembering the first time he told her that.

"You don't look so bad yourself."

He placed the velvet box on the table near the door.

"The flowers are from Jerome," Dix said opening the plastic box. "Here is yours."

He asked for her wrist and slipped on a corsage of white roses with green leaves and baby's breath all tied together with a green velvet bow.

Dix held up the other one. "Evie, this one's for you."

Dix handed the remaining corsage made of coral and white roses with a silver ribbon to Pops. Her grandfather hesitated.

"Heathcliff, you promised to be nice for the entire evening. Jerome went to the trouble of getting this, now put it on me."

Pops grumbled something under his breath but from where Meg stood, she couldn't quite hear him.

Dix picked up the black velvet box. "I got you a little something for Christmas but seeing as though I won't be here, I thought you'd like to wear them tonight with your gown."

Meg's hands shook as she opened it. Inside, nestled in black velour, was a pair of earrings. Petite white gold butterflies dangled with tiny diamonds and at the end of each diamond, a tear-shaped emerald.

"Oh, Dix, they're exquisite."

Gran came over and peeked inside the box. "They match your dress perfectly." She winked at Dix.

"Dix went through all the trouble to pick them out just for you, Meg. What are you waiting for? Put them on."

She went over to the mirror in the foyer and fastened them to her ears. When she moved her head from side to side, the light caught the tiny diamonds making them sparkle like stars in an inky sky.

"Thank you, Dix."

He moved closer to her. " Merry Christmas."

Dix drove the Darlings to the ball. Once they arrived, Gran walked through the door on Pops' arm. Megan watched as Jerry and her grandparents all made eye contact. Gran wasted no time in leading Pops and Jerry to a quiet room away from prying eyes and ears. People in the crowd murmured when the three members of the love triangle disappeared down the corridor.

"Do you think they'll be okay?" Dix asked taking her jacket.

"They'll be fine. Gran will play mediator, and everything will get worked out. It might take more than one evening, but it will."

Noah ran by with Ethan and Charlie, who'd arrived earlier. Mostly everyone Jerry invited, came, no doubt just to get a look inside the mansion. Meg only hoped it would raise the money for Jerry's foundation the way Jerry hoped it would.

Dix took Meg by the hand.

"It's our last night together until after the holidays, and I'm not letting you out of my sight all night. Let's dance."

Meg had loved her time with Dix and Noah. She could picture herself with the two of them living happily ever after as Dix's wife and Noah's step-mother but thoughts like that were the stuff of fairy tales. People didn't fall in love in a few weeks' time. Reality would return tomorrow when Dix and Noah left for California. And reality sucked.

The good thing was, Pops and Jerry had worked things out. At one point, Meg glanced over and Jerry and Pops laughed out loud at a private joke.

When the musicians played The Christmas Waltz, Gran danced with Jerry. The rest of the night Gran and Pops shared a few dances together.

Meg stood near the Christmas tree in the ballroom, her cheeks hot from the spiked eggnog she sipped on. Dix had gone to get his drink refreshed but returned and stood behind her.

"What are you looking at?" he asked.

"I've been watching the three of them." Gran, Pops, and Jerome sat in a semi-circle, Jerry in his scooter, and her grandparents each on an armchair. "They're laughing a lot, which is good."

"It's great to see Jerome so happy," Dix said.

"It is. I hope they keep in touch after this. It would be good for all three of them."

"Come on," Dix said, taking her hand. He led her into the

library, the place where she first got acquainted with the Graham family. She went to the window and looked out. The Christmas lights they put up on the trees in the front of the mansion reflected off the snow and sparkled. In the distance, the lights that were hung on the outside of the Christmas Loft and the house twinkled, too. Meg wondered how many times over the years Jerry sat there looking down at their farm and tears sprang to her eyes. Jerry could have had love if he chose to. And if she chose to believe Dix's promise that he'd return, she could have it too.

Dix kissed her lightly on the back of her neck and wrapped her arms around her waist, sending goosebumps down her left side. "I'm going to miss this," he said, kissing the other side of her neck, causing the same reaction.

Meg turned to face him. "I'm not great with goodbyes, Dix."

Dix lowered his head and she closed her eyes. His kisses always made her swoon and now that this thing between them was almost over, she returned his kiss with all the urgency and desperation of a woman who would never again see the guy who she dreamed might possibly be the love of her life.

"This isn't goodbye, Meg. I'll be back."

"If you make promises like that, I'm apt to believe them. And I can't do that, Dix."

Dix kissed her over and over until Noah burst into the room.

"There you are," Noah said, out of breath from running. "Pops and Gran want to leave now, Meg."

Dix drove them all home. Gran helped Pops inside while Dix walked her to the door. Her grandparents went off to bed while she and Dix stood in the foyer, holding onto each other for a long while until he gave her one more kiss that warmed her against the winter air.

He went out of the door, leaving her breathless and shaking, the way his kisses always left her. But neither one of them said goodbye. They didn't need to. Their kisses, the ones Meg never wanted to end, had done that for them.

· · ·

The next week, Meg tried not to dwell on the fact that she missed Dixon and Noah. They texted every day, but as it got closer to Christmas, their conversations became less and less, just like she knew they would. Life had returned to the way it was before Dixon and Noah came to Chelsea, leaving her heart aching and empty with no idea how to fix it.

She kept herself occupied. The farm opened at eleven every day during the week and nine on the weekends. At night, she had choir practice at the church at the urging of her other bestie, Maureen, the church's music and choir director.

Three days before Christmas, Meg walked from the Christmas Loft to the house for lunch and heard raucous laughter as she neared the back door.

Jerry sat at the table with Gran and Pops.

Meg greeted him with a kiss and a hug.

"What are you doing here, Jerry?"

"That big house is too quiet now that Dixon and Noah are gone. At the ball, Evie and Cliff invited me for lunch and here I am."

Gran had even invited him to Christmas dinner, and he'd accepted.

As time went on, Meg still missed the guys since they'd gone back home but her heart remained steadfast in the fact that she had no regrets about she and Dix becoming intimate.

In time, she'd be able to date again. She'd dipped her toe into the dating pool once again and that had been the whole purpose of their fling in the first place.

She arrived at the church the night before Christmas Eve for one last choir rehearsal.

The crowd of choir members chatted amongst themselves until Meg walked over. A hush came over the crowd.

"Well, this is awkward," Meg said.

Maureen put an arm around Meg's shoulders. "I need your help."

"What kind of help?"

"Singing."

"Oh, boy."

Mo went on to explain that Father Kelly had the flu and he wouldn't be able to sing his part in the Gesu Bambino song, something he'd done since he came to their parish a few years ago.

"And what does that have to do with me?"

"You're the best singer we've got for that part."

"Oh no, Mo. I'm much better as the voice of many, which is why I sing in a *choir*."

Mo rolled her eyes. "Look, Meg, I'm already stressed out, and I don't have time to argue with you about this. Here's the sheet music. Just do it."

Meg didn't have a choice when Mo put it like that. Besides, her young cousin Charlie had the lead for the kid's choir so together with him, she'd put on her big girl pants and did what Mo told her. She'd sung the song with the choir, just not the solo.

Her stomach buzzed like bees in a hive from nerves all day on Christmas Eve, thinking about that solo. The rehearsals sounded okay, but she always doubted herself.

On her way back to the church, Meg took a deep breath and enjoyed the scene around her. It had snowed earlier but stopped before the sun went down leaving a sugar coating of the white stuff on everything. Meg had texted Dix to wish him a Merry Christmas. He never texted back but she always forgot about the time difference. She was content with the way they left things. He kept saying he'd be back, but she'd believe it if it happened.

And he'd text her back when he got around to it. He always did.

Meg arrived at church and felt less like throwing up as she mingled with other choir members. The mass began and the choir's first song was Hark the Herald Angels Sing.

Father Miller, the priest that came to fill in for Father Kelly, moved things right along. Poor Father Miller. Meg had asked Mo why she hadn't asked him to sing Father Kelly's part in the song. Mo informed her that she had but discovered through an unfortunate audition that the poor man was tone-deaf. Mo immediately put the kibosh on that idea.

Finally, during communion, it was time for Meg's solo. She stepped forward and began singing the opening measures.

*"When blossoms flowered 'mid the snow, upon a
winter night..."*

She completed the first verse and while the choir came in, she could finally breathe again—until something caught her eye. She tilted her head to get a better view of the pews to her left.

Jerry sat on the aisle in his motorized scooter. Next to him was Noah and next to him... Dixon.

Meg almost lost her place in the music, but once Charlie began his part, she picked it up. Questions spun through her mind, making it hard to concentrate. What were they doing here? She managed to get through the song and the rest of the mass.

When it was over, she waded through the crowd of people who came to congratulate her on her performance. She graciously thanked everyone but needed to see Dix.

Finally, the crowd dispersed enough for her to get through. Dix stood a couple of feet away from her. Meg picked up the bottom of her choir robe and ran the rest of the way into his arms.

"I thought I was seeing things," she said.

"I told you I'd be back."

"You said after the holidays."

He kissed the top of her head. "Noah and I wanted to surprise you."

"You and Charlie sing great together, Meg." Noah hugged her and she gave him a giant squeeze and kissed the top of his head.

"Thanks, Bud."

Meg rode with Dix while Noah rode with her cousins back to the farm. Dix held her hand the whole way and Meg couldn't stop smiling. When she tried to exit the car, he grasped her hand.

"Let's go to the loft, Meg."

She didn't think twice. She hurried there, throwing open the door then flipping on the propane fireplace, before hurrying up the ladder with Dix behind her.

He sat on the bed and pulled her down onto his lap.

"This is the best Christmas present ever," she said, kissing him.

"When we returned home, I started getting things in order to come back here, but I couldn't concentrate on anything. All I did was think about you and our time together. I've never been happier than when I was here with you. And all poor Noah did was mope around."

"I missed you guys, too. But what about your business? Was that enough time to get everything straightened out?"

"Didn't Jerome tell you?"

"Tell me what?" Her pulse raced in anticipation.

"He hired a lawyer to take care of all of that so we could come back here sooner. It makes sense. That way Noah can start at the school here in Chelsea right after the holiday break. And I'm going to set up an office at the mansion."

Her heart soared. She had kept her guard up, not allowing herself to hope he'd return.

She threw her arms around his neck. He brushed his lips across her temple then lifted her chin up to look into her eyes.

"I know it's a lot to ask after only knowing each other for a month. I also know I have Noah so that means I come with a ready-made family, but it feels right, Meg. I haven't had a serious relationship with anyone in a very long time, but I'd like to make an honest try at having one with you. What do you say?"

"I can't wait to start." She kissed him again.

"Merry Christmas, Meg."

"It is now," she said, kissing him deeply as he laid her back on the bed.

About the Author

Sera Cassell is addicted to writing fun, steamy romance with feisty heroines and the swoon-worthy heroes who fall for them. Her books always have a happy ending and more than likely, a nod to her Irish/Scottish heritage.

She is living her own happily ever after in New England with her adrenaline junkie husband, three daughters and two grand-daughters. She is also pet mom to two mini dachshunds, Darla and Spanky, and Poly, her polydactyl cat.

When she's not spending time with her girl tribe, she enjoys reading, eating New Haven pizza, sipping London Fog tea lattes, and binging on chocolate. Any kind. She's never met a piece of chocolate she doesn't like.

www.ingramcontent.com/pod-product-compliance
Lightning Source LLC
Chambersburg PA
CBHW061331120726
48001CB00002B/786